DOCTOR WHO
THE THREE DOCTORS

THE CHANGING FACE OF DOCTOR WHO

The cover illustration portrays the first,
second and third Doctors.

Also available in the Target series:

DOCTOR WHO
THE THREE
DOCTORS

Based on the BBC television serial *The Three Doctors* by Robert Baker and Dave Martin by arrangement with the British Broadcasting Corporation.

TERRANCE DICKS

TARGET

Target Books is a division of Tandem Publishing
Ltd., 14 Gloucester Road, London SW7 4RD

A Howard & Wyndham Company

First published in Great Britain by Tandem
Publishing Ltd., 1975
Second impression 1976

ISBN 0 426 11578 3

Printed in Great Britain by The Anchor Press Ltd.,
and bound by Wm. Brendon & Son Ltd.,
both of Tiptree, Essex

Contents

Lightning from Space

For an adventure that was to be one of the most astonishing of the Doctor's very long life, it all began very quietly. It started, in fact, with a silvery-grey balloon, drifting peacefully out of the blue morning sky to land on the flat marshy ground of an Essex bird sanctuary. Hanging from the balloon was a bright orange box, about the size and shape of a car battery.

The box bumped along the ground as a gust of wind caught in the balloon. Then its attaching wires caught fast in a clump of trees, and sent a flock of starlings shrieking into the sky.

On the other side of the trees a stocky grey-haired man, in anorak and rubber boots, paused to listen. Arthur Hollis was the warden of the Bird sanctuary, and he knew at once, by the note of outrage in the starlings' voices, that something unusual had happened. He made his way round the trees, and saw the brightly coloured box swinging to and fro like a stranded parachutist. He walked up to it cautiously. As he got closer he saw thick black letters on the side of the box. They read: 'Reward! Please Contact Dr. Tyler.' An address and telephone number followed. Hollis rubbed his chin. He didn't like mysterious objects turning up in his bird sanctuary.

The sooner it was out of there the better. He copied the telephone number on a scrap of paper. Suddenly the box *crackled*. Hollis jumped back. He looked at it cautiously. Nothing happened. Shaking his head suspiciously, Hollis gave the box a last distrustful glare and set off for his cottage.

Several hours later, a battered and muddy Land Rover jolted down the bumpy lane to the bird sanctuary. It was driven by a tubby, fair-haired little man in an old duffle-coat. He pulled up outside the Warden's cottage and got out.

A pleasant-looking middle-aged woman in an apron came down the cottage path. 'Dr. Tyler, is it? From the University?'

Tyler nodded. 'That's me. Sorry to be a trouble. Thanks very much for calling—'

The woman interrupted him, her voice a little anxious. 'That old box of yours is just through the trees there.' She pointed across the fields to a small hill. Tyler could just see the silver-grey of the balloon as it caught the sunlight. 'My Arthur's keeping an eye on it for you,' she went on. 'He hasn't touched it. Not chemicals, I hope? Only, it's the birds, you see. He took his shot-gun in case it was dangerous.'

Tyler shook his head vigorously. 'No, nothing like that. Just instruments. Thanks very much, Mrs. Hollis, I'll go and find your husband.' He set off towards the trees at an eager pace. As he approached the hill, he called out, 'Mr. Hollis! Mr. Hollis!'

He saw Hollis appear over the brow of the hill, wave

and point downwards. The box was obviously on the other side, just out of sight.

Vastly relieved that the mysterious object would soon be off his hands, Hollis decided to speed the process by unhooking it from the tree, where it was still swinging gently to and fro. It took him only a moment to free the clamps attaching the box to its wires, but the box was surprisingly heavy, and as he took the full weight of it he stumbled forwards, and fell on top of the box as it hit the ground. There was a sudden fierce crackle, a flash of light, and Arthur Hollis vanished.

Tyler came puffing over the hill. The balloon still flapped about in the tree top, the box rested at the foot of the tree. But of Arthur Hollis there was no sign. Tyler looked round unbelievingly. He'd *seen* the man just a minute ago. And there was nowhere he could be hiding—just flat, empty fields all around. Tyler walked up to the box and looked at it. Just the familiar type of instrument box he'd handled a hundred times before. Heaving it up, he clasped it to his chest and set off for the cottage at a stumbling run.

Later that day, the box was sitting on a laboratory bench while Tyler, for what seemed the hundredth time, explained what had happened.

'So there you are. Mrs. Hollis says her husband's *with* the box. I *see* him wave, get there, and there he is—gone! So I phone the police, and they whizz me off to see you lot.'

Tyler looked round at his audience. There were

three of them. A very small, very pretty, fair-haired girl. A tall man with a clipped moustache, wearing the uniform of a Brigadier. And an even taller man, flamboyantly dressed in a velvet smoking-jacket and ruffled shirt, who seemed to be known only as 'the Doctor'.

Brigadier Alastair Lethbridge-Stewart, head of the British section of the United Nations Intelligence Task-force (UNIT for short), beamed approvingly. 'Quite right too, that's what we're here for—eh, Doctor?'

The Doctor gave him an enigmatic look and said nothing. Jo Grant, the Doctor's assistant, was examining the box that was the centre of attention. 'Dr. Tyler,' she asked suddenly, 'what's it *for*?'

The Brigadier frowned at her disapprovingly, and then realised he didn't really know the answer himself. He looked at Tyler enquiringly.

The little man seemed surprised that anyone should need to ask. 'Cosmic-ray research, of course.' He gave the box a tap. 'In there is the most sophisticated cosmic-ray monitoring device between here and Cape Kennedy.' He flashed them a sudden, disarming grin. 'I ought to know because I knocked it up myself from odds and ends in the lab. As a matter of fact . . .' Tyler hesitated awkwardly.

The Doctor gave him an encouraging smile. 'As a matter of fact, what?' he asked gently.

'Well, I'd been meaning to get in touch with some-body official anyway, even before this business.'

'And why was that?'

Tyler took a deep breath, then seemed to come to some kind of decision. 'Pass me that briefcase, will you, young lady?' Jo Grant passed over the bulging briefcase Tyler had brought with him, staggering under the unexpected weight. Tyler fished out a sheaf of papers, all mixed up with what looked like X-ray prints. 'We've been getting some pretty amazing results on these latest tests.' He sorted out one of the prints and handed it to the Doctor, who held it up to the light. Jo peered at it too. All she could see was a scattering of tiny white spots against the darkness of the negative.

'There's an early one, d'you see,' said Tyler. 'Just your average-density cosmic-ray bombardment. But on the last one, we got this!' He handed over another print. The Doctor held it up, and this time Jo saw what looked like a jagged sheet of lightning slashing right across the print. She heard the Doctor's sudden intake of breath. 'Good grief!'

'Aye,' said Tyler grimly. 'And now take a look at these!' He handed the Doctor a tattered roll of papers covered with figures. Jo guessed that they were computer print-outs of some kind.

A moment later the Doctor looked up. 'If these readings are correct, Dr. Tyler, this—whatever-it-is —travels faster than light!'

'That's right,' said Tyler simply. 'And it can't, can it?' He looked up at the Doctor's tall figure. 'I don't know what to make of it, Doctor, and that's the truth. You know what it makes me think of? A shriek of pain, travelling across the Galaxy! It's come all that way, through millions of star systems. It must have been— directed. Directed at *us*! Why?'

Gently the Doctor put the prints back on the bench.

'Why indeed, Dr. Tyler!' He took a fresh batch of print-outs from Tyler, and began poring over them, quite oblivious to everything else.

The Brigadier cleared his throat meaningfully. What had started off as a fairly straightforward disappearance seemed to have wandered off into the realms of cosmic-ray research. 'The point is, Doctor, has this space-lightning of yours got anything to do with the vanishing of this chap Hollis?'

'Oh I should think so, wouldn't you?' The Doctor looked up at the Brigadier, and then back at the prints on the bench. 'Space-lightning . . . you know, that's rather good, Brigadier. It does look a bit like lightning.'

The Brigadier looked pleased, then was immediately deflated as the Doctor went on, 'Only of course it isn't lightning. Nothing like it.'

'Do you know what it is, Doctor?' asked Jo.

'Well, if there were such a thing, I should say it was compressed light. Yes that's it—a sort of controlled superlucent emission.'

The Brigadier sighed. He was used to the fact that most of the Doctor's explanations left him none the wiser.

The Doctor leaped to his feet. 'Mr. Tyler, is this cosmic-ray device of yours functioning normally?'

'As far as I know. Haven't developed the plate yet of course.'

'Then I suggest you do so at once. I think you'll find all the necessary equipment over there. If you need anything else, the Brigadier will get it for you. Come along, Jo.'

Obediently, Jo started to follow the Doctor. The Brigadier snapped, 'May I ask where you're off to?'

'To take a look at the scene of the disappearance, of course.' The Doctor grabbed his cloak from behind the door and set off. Jo gave the Brigadier a 'What-can-you-do?' look, and hurried after him.

Tyler wandered over to the cupboard indicated by the Doctor and opened it. The shelves were crammed with every kind of scientific equipment. He spotted one of the latest types of automatic developer, fished it out, carried it over to a bench and started checking it over. Looking up, he saw the Brigadier glaring down at him.

'All right, old chap, I can manage,' said Tyler kindly. 'I'll give you a shout if I need anything.'

The Brigadier seemed to be controlling himself with an effort. 'That's very kind of you, Dr. Tyler,' he said between gritted teeth. 'Do make yourself at home. Liberty Hall, Dr. Tyler, Liberty Hall!' Slamming the door behind him, the Brigadier marched off down the corridor.

Tyler shook his head in mild astonishment. Funny chap, that. Still, you could never tell with soldiers. Peculiar lot.

Satisfied that the developer was in working order, Tyler carefully extracted the plate from the orange box and slipped it inside. There was a low hum as he switched on the developer, and a few minutes later, the print popped out of the machine. Tyler held it up to the light, and almost dropped it from sheer surprise. The same jagged streak ran across the print. But it was superimposed across the blurred picture of a

13

screaming face. It was a face Tyler had seen before, though only for a few seconds—that of the vanished Arthur Hollis.

Tyler shook his head, trying to keep his grasp on reality. 'That shouldn't happen,' he muttered. 'That shouldn't happen at all.' He went back to the orange box and started to undo the clamps and screws which held on the lid. His fingers carried out the familiar process automatically, his mind still grappling with the mystery of what he had just seen. He began taking out pieces of electronic equipment and laying them on the bench. Then he saw there was something else in the box. Huddled in one corner was what looked like a blob of jelly. Tyler reached and poked it. There was a sudden fierce crackle. Like Arthur Hollis before him, Tyler vanished.

For a moment the blob of jelly lay inert in the corner of the box. Then it climbed slowly up the side, quivered on the edge, and plopped down on the laboratory bench. At first it was motionless, as if puzzled by the new environment. Then it slid along the bench, dropped into the little sink and vanished down the plug-hole. The laboratory was empty.

The Doctor, Jo Grant and Mrs. Hollis trudged up to the top of the little hill and paused for breath. Mrs. Hollis pointed.

'There's your old balloon, down there.' They could see the silvery shape flapping about in the breeze, still tethered to its tree. The Doctor nodded, and they walked down the hill towards it.

At the foot of the tree the Doctor immediately started casting about, reminding Jo irresistibly of a hound looking for a scent. Fishing in his pockets he produced a gadget rather like a miniature geiger-counter, and started testing the area. Jo saw he was totally absorbed, and turned to Mrs. Hollis. She was watching the Doctor with an indulgent smile, like a mother who sees her child occupied with his new chemistry set. 'Mrs. Hollis,' asked Jo, 'I don't suppose there's been any sign of your husband—since this morning?'

'No, m'dear, that there hasn't. Still, nothing unusual in that!'

'You're not worried, then?'

'Bless you, why should I be? My Arthur's gone off somewhere. We shan't see him now till dark.'

'Dr. Tyler did say he'd disappeared.'

Mrs. Hollis chuckled placidly. 'No doubt he did. You see, my Arthur, he's a bit of a shy one. Don't take to strangers much. He'll have pointed out the balloon, then slipped away quiet-like.'

'Wouldn't Dr. Tyler have seen him?'

'See my Arthur? Not if he didn't want him to!'

Jo sighed. Could it all be as simple as that? Was Arthur Hollis placidly watching his birds on some distant part of the reserve? She looked down at the Doctor. Crouched on one knee, he was slowly moving his instrument over a little patch of ground. Jo saw the dials flicker, and, very faintly, she thought she heard a crackle.

The Doctor straightened up, and put his instrument

back in his pocket. 'Thank you for all your help, Mrs. Hollis. We'd better be going now.'

As they walked back towards the cottage, Mrs. Hollis said helpfully, 'If you really need to see my Arthur, I could try to find him for you.'

The Doctor said, 'Never mind, Mrs. Hollis, it isn't that important.'

Outside the little cottage they said goodbye to Mrs. Hollis, climbed into 'Bessie', the Doctor's Edwardian roadster, and drove off. Jo looked at the Doctor. He was driving fast but carefully, as he always did, but she could see that his mind was far away. 'It is, important, isn't it, Doctor—whatever happened back there?'

'Far more important than I'd realised.'

'What were you testing for with that gadget? Radioactivity?'

'No. Anti-matter,' replied the Doctor briefly.

'What's that?'

'Something that can't exist—not in this Universe anyway.'

In that case why look for it? thought Jo. But she could see the Doctor was in no mood for further questions.

At UNIT H.Q., the Brigadier had a lot of questions, and he wasn't getting answers to any of them. Feeling a little contrite at the abrupt way he'd spoken to Dr. Tyler—after all it wasn't Tyler's fault if the Doctor was so irritating—the Brigadier had popped back to the laboratory to ask the little man how he was getting on. But Doctor Tyler seemed to have vanished. A thorough check of the building had produced no sign of him, and the Brigadier sat irritably tapping a pencil on his desk, wondering how he was going to explain a mysterious disappearance from his own headquarters. Sergeant Benton popped his head cautiously round the door. 'Report from the main gate, sir. The Doctor's just appeared.'

'Well tell him his friend Tyler's just *disappeared*— and ask him to come and see me right away.' Benton withdrew his head and went to look for the Doctor, thankful for an excuse to get out of the Brigadier's immediate vicinity.

The Doctor, meanwhile, was driving Bessie into UNIT's extensive car park. He swung his long legs over the side of the little car. 'Come on, Jo, let's see if Tyler learned anything from that machine of his.'

Obediently Jo scrambled out after him, and they started walking towards the main building. As usual, the Doctor's longer strides took him in front of Jo, and she was running to catch up when she heard a sudden crackle. She stopped, listened. The crackle came again. It was coming from one of the drains at the side of the building. Something was coming out of it . . . a big blob of some kind of jelly, about the size of a football. It was shot through with iridescent colours, like a patch of oil on a wet pavement. And it was hard to focus your eyes on, as if in some strange way it wasn't quite *there*. Yet it *was* there. Rubbing her eyes, staring with a kind of fascinated horror, Jo backed away.

She tried to call out, but her voice seemed stuck in her throat. 'Doctor,' she croaked, 'Doctor!'

The blob of jelly seemed to react to the sound of her voice. With a threatening crackle it began moving towards her . . .

2

Attack from the Unknown

Jo screamed, and the Doctor turned to see what was the matter. She was backing away, the blob of jelly slithering remorselessly after her. The Doctor called, 'Jo—stand still.' With considerable effort, Jo forced herself to stop. The blob stopped too. Then, as the Doctor moved cautiously towards it, the blob changed direction, and started rolling slowly towards *him*. 'Jo,' he called, 'do exactly as I say. Start backing away slowly towards the door.'

Jo obeyed. The Doctor meanwhile began to circle cautiously around the blob, doing his best to lead it away from Jo. Unerringly the blob followed his every change of direction almost, as if it was tracking him. Jo called shakily, 'Doctor, what *is* that thing?'

'Never mind that now. When I tell you to run— run!'

The Doctor started manoeuvring round his car, so that 'Bessie' was between him and the blob. 'Now, Jo, run!' he yelled. Jo sprinted for the door. For a moment the blob hesitated, as if wondering whether to follow her. Then, with terrifying speed, it made a sudden rush at the Doctor. As the blob shot towards 'Bessie', the Doctor ducked round the other side of the little car and sprinted after Jo. She was hesitating by the open door, reluctant to abandon him, when the Doctor hurtled through and, scooping Jo up before him, slammed the door shut and bolted it from the other side. As he did so a bright, silent flash came from behind them. They looked through the glass panel in the upper part of the door. The Doctor's little roadster had simply vanished. They were just in time to see the blob of jelly slither across the garage floor and disappear down the drain from which it had first appeared.

The Brigadier looked up impatiently as Benton entered the office.

'Well?' he snapped.

Benton swallowed hard. 'Still no sign of Dr. Tyler, sir. I've re-checked the entire building. He's certainly not inside, but all the gate sentries swear he hasn't left.'

'What about *our* Doctor—or have you managed to lose him as well?'

The Brigadier's phone rang, and he snatched it up. Somehow he felt sure that it would be more bad news. He was not disappointed. He listened to the excited voice at the other end of the phone. 'What do you mean?' he barked. 'An explosion in the garage? I heard nothing . . .'

To Benton's relief the Doctor chose that moment to walk in. He looked calm and unruffled—which was more than could be said for Jo Grant, who followed close behind him. The Brigadier looked up. 'Ah there you are! Apparently there was some kind of flash . . .'

'There was indeed,' agreed the Doctor.

'What happened? One of your gadgets misfire?'

The Doctor frowned. 'I'm not really sure, yet. Let's say there was an energy-release of some kind.'

'There was this horrible great blob of jelly,' Jo burst out, 'and Bessie's just vanished . . .' She gave an excited report of events in the garage.

When she had finished the Brigadier gazed at her in stark disbelief. He looked at the Doctor for confirmation. The Doctor nodded. 'A rather incoherent account, but substantially correct.'

'We've been having a little mystery of our own,' said the Brigadier grimly. He went on to tell the Doctor about the vanishing of Dr. Tyler.

The Doctor seemed unsurprised. 'I shouldn't bother to look for him any more. I'm very much afraid he's gone where Mr. Hollis went. Where Bessie's gone too, come to that.'

The Brigadier struggled on valiantly. 'What about this jelly—this thing that attacked you in the garage? What is it? Where does it fit in with all this business about Hollis and Dr. Tyler?'

The Doctor dropped into a chair, swinging his long legs up to rest his heels on the Brigadier's desk-top. 'As far as I can guess—and it *is* only a guess so far— the jelly, thing, as you call it, is some kind of organism. An organism with a powerful hunting instinct. I believe it travelled to Earth by means of Dr. Tyler's "space-lightning", using his cosmic-ray device for the last stage of the journey.'

'Sort of like hitching a lift?' suggested Jo brightly. Everyone ignored her.

'All that's as may be,' snapped the Brigadier. 'What

concerns us now is that the thing's here. Why? What does it want?'

The Doctor cleared his throat. 'I hate to sound immodest,' he said gently,' but I'm very much afraid it wants *me*.'

The Brigadier looked at him in exasperation. 'Are you seriously trying to tell me, Doctor, that this whole thing has been arranged for your benefit?'

'In the garage,' said Jo slowly, 'as soon as it got near you, it ignored me.'

The Brigadier got up. 'Well, whatever it is, it's arrived and it's hostile. What do we do? How do we find it?'

The Doctor, too, rose to his feet. 'No need for us to try and find it, Brigadier. If we wait, it will find us.'

In the darkness of the drainage system under the UNIT building the blob of jelly lay motionless, waiting. Suddenly it began to glow and crackle with energy. And it started to grow. As it grew, it divided into two. Each of those two pieces divided yet again. The process continued. Two pieces, four pieces, eight pieces, sixteen pieces, thirty-two pieces . . . Soon an army of them swarmed through the drainage pipes, making their way towards the surface . . .

In a quiet side-road at the back of UNIT H.Q., a glowing, crackling blob of jelly emerged from a drain. For a moment it lay in the gutter, then it started to grow, swelling to the size of a man. As it grew, it changed, taking on roughly, very roughly, the *shape* of a man. A huge figure with round featureless head and thick blobby arms and legs, it stood motionless for a moment, then began shambling purposefully towards UNIT. A moment later another blob of jelly emerged crackling from the drain. It too began to grow and change shape. Before very long, a second nightmarish creature lurched off after the first.

All round the UNIT building, the same process was being repeated. The blobs of jelly emerged from drains, grew, changed shape, and began their remorseless advance. Before very long a hideous, shambling, monstrous army was encircling UNIT H.Q., moving in closer and closer.

The main gate sentry saw them first, and frankly didn't believe his eyes. A quivering line of faceless horrors marched steadily towards him. Too astonished to challenge them, or even to give the alarm, he simply opened fire at the nearest with his Sterling submachine gun. It didn't help. He *saw* the bullets slice through the jelly-like substance of the creatures' bodies. They continued their advance without even a pause.

Corporal Palmer, in charge of the guard, ran out from his guard-room at the sound of the shooting. He saw the terrified sentry, too frightened even to reload, clutching an empty gun and backing slowly away. Shoving the soldier in front of him, he dashed back into the guard-room and sounded the General Alarm siren. Its harsh wailing note set the whole building in motion. Soldiers carrying arms ran at once to their battle stations, those without made for the armoury, where the Armourer was already issuing rifles, grenades and Sterlings.

Sergeant Benton used his rank to jump the queue and grabbed an anti-tank rifle. Experience of hostile alien life-forms had taught him that the heavier your armament the better. Shouldering the cumbersome weapon with ease, he ran to see what the blazes was going on.

All around the building he found a weird battle taking place. The terrifying jelly-creatures were swarming everywhere, ignoring the fusillade of shots being poured into them. Yet despite their fearsome appearance, they didn't seem to hurt you unless you touched them. As Benton ran up to the main gate, he saw a terrified soldier stumble into one of them. A crackle of energy threw the man a good twenty feet, smashing him into the wall.

Dropping to one knee, Benton levelled his anti-tank gun and fired. With a dull 'crump' the explosive shell blasted the jelly-creature into a hundred pieces. Benton smiled in satisfaction—then he saw the little blobs of jelly roll back together into a great blob, and the creature start moving towards him once more. Dodging out of its way, he grabbed for his walkie-talkie.

In the Doctor's laboratory, Jo Grant listened as Benton's voice came through on the field-radio. From all around she could hear the rattle of gunfire, the sound of exploding grenades. She looked across at the Doctor. Absorbed in a batch of Tyler's computer print-outs, he seemed to be ignoring the whole battle.

She heard the Brigadier say, 'All right, Sergeant Benton, move the men out. Complete evacuation!'

He turned to the Doctor, and snapped, 'Doctor, for heaven's sake! We're under attack. What are these creatures? Where do they come from?'

The Doctor looked up. 'Obviously from the same source as that thing in the garage. First the scout, then the reinforcements. Sound grasp of military tactics, wouldn't you say, Brigadier?'

The Brigadier exploded. 'Never mind all that—what do we *do*?'

'Nothing,' said the Doctor calmly. 'They're not interested in you or your men. Keep out of their way and they won't harm you.'

'What about you, Doctor?'

The Doctor nodded at the TARDIS in the corner. 'Don't worry, I'll be all right. You go and look after your men, Brigadier.'

This was a suggestion the Brigadier found hard to refuse. The safety of his men was always his first concern.

'Very well, Doctor, if you're sure. Come along, Miss Grant.' The Brigadier ran out of the room. Jo didn't move.

The Doctor said gently, 'I really think *you* ought to leave as well, Jo.'

She shook her head determinedly. 'And walk into one of those nasties? Not a chance, I'm staying with you.'

'Please, Jo. It's only when you *are* with me that you're in any danger. On your own you can walk straight by them and they'll ignore you.'

The ground-floor window was thrown up, and Sergeant Benton climbed over the sill. 'Doctor, Miss

Grant,' he yelled. 'You've got to get out of here. Those things are making straight for the lab.'

The Doctor picked Jo up bodily and carried her across to the window.

'On the contrary, Sergeant Benton, *you* get out of here. And take Miss Grant with you, if you have to carry her!'

He tried to pass Jo over to Benton. She said, 'Oh no you don't' and started struggling wildly. Before they could all untangle themselves, there was a sudden flash and the laboratory door disappeared.

A milling crowd of the jelly-creatures at once filled the empty space. They had already begun to recombine, merging into one another to form a huge blob, a larger version of the one that had attacked them in the garage. It was as though, their target found, they no longer needed their ghastly attempt at a human shape.

Another blob, equally large, appeared at the window, cutting off their retreat. As the two masses of jelly lurched towards them the Doctor ran to the TARDIS and unlocked the door. 'Into the TARDIS, both of you,' he snapped. He bundled Jo and Sergeant Benton inside, then leaped in after them, shutting the TARDIS door just as the combined mass of jelly slammed against it.

Inside the TARDIS the Doctor ran to the control console and started flicking switches. With its usual groaning sound the centre column began moving up and down.

Jo looked surprised. 'I thought the TARDIS was grounded, Doctor?'

'So it is! But while it's ticking over, the force-field is in operation.' Jo suddenly noticed Sergeant Benton, who was standing quite still, his eyes wide open, his mouth clamped shut. She realised it was the first time he had ever been inside the TARDIS, and smiled sympathetically. She could well remember how she'd felt on first seeing the big gleaming control room that was so impossibly packed inside the battered old police box. The Doctor followed the direction of her glance. He too smiled to see the big Sergeant standing almost to attention with astonishment. 'Well,' asked the Doctor briskly, 'aren't you going to say "It's bigger on the inside than on the outside"? Everyone else does.'

Benton made an effort to keep his voice steady. 'That's pretty obvious, isn't it? Anyway, nothing to do with you surprises me now, Doc!'

The Doctor chuckled, went across to the console and switched on the scanner screen. The others gathered round him, looking at the scene inside the laboratory. The jelly-creature, all its parts now combined into one enormous lump, was lashing to and fro, throwing out occasional tentacles, rather like a giant amoeba. Whenever it touched the TARDIS it recoiled with an angry crackle, but whenever it touched anything else there was a fierce silent flash, and that object vanished. Chairs, desk, laboratory benches, cupboards, they all went, until the laboratory was virtually empty. Except, that is, for the TARDIS, which still sat stubbornly in its corner.

Jo looked away from the screen with a shudder. 'What's it *doing*, Doctor?'

'Trying to carry out its instructions, I imagine, and

getting in a rare old tizzy because it can't.' The Doctor opened a concealed hatch in the console. Beneath it was a tiny red button. He looked at it for a long time, and sighed. 'It's no good. I'll have to use it.' Almost as if forcing himself, he pressed the little button and closed the hatch.

'Use what?' asked Jo, curiously.

'The SOS—this is one of the very few times in my life when I've had to ask Them for help.'

Jo knew that the Doctor was talking about his own race, the mysterious all-powerful Time Lords. It was by their decree that he was presently exiled to Earth, and to have to ask for their help must have cost him a great deal. She said, 'Things must be pretty serious then.'

The Doctor looked at the scanner screen, which showed the angry jelly-monster still thrashing angrily about in the empty laboratory.

'They are, Jo. Very serious indeed. The whole of the Universe is in danger!'

3

The Menace of the Black Hole

On a monitor screen, millions of light-years away across the galaxies, the Doctor's SOS showed up as a tiny blinking light. The monitor was one of many in the vast Temporal Control Room of the Time Lords. It was many years since the Doctor had stood in that room. If he could have seen it at this moment, he would have been shocked and horrified.

Usually the Temporal Control Room was a busy bustling place, hundreds of monitor screens glowing brightly, Time Lords moving around busily as they carried out their work of charting the Time Streams of the Universe, keeping a benevolent and watchful eye on innumerable planets and times. But now the huge hall was in semi-darkness, only a few of the Temporal Monitors were still in operation, their lights glowing faintly in the surrounding gloom. Across the almost empty hall walked two Senior Time Lords, the President of the High Council and his Chancellor. Their appearance would have given the Doctor the greatest shock of all. Despite their age and wisdom, the Senior Time Lords had always been lively, vigorous figures, burning with energy and authority. But this was true no longer. Under the dignity of the flowing, ornamental robes were two tired and frightened old men.

The Chancellor looked at the winking light of the Doctor's signal. 'The Doctor is still holding out?'

The President nodded sadly. 'We were about to seek his help. Now *he* asks for *ours*. And we have none to give him.'

The Chancellor brooded for a moment. 'And the source of our present energy loss—it is still under observation?'

The President led him to another monitor nearby. This screen showed a panorama of deep space, filled with thousands of stars. But at the centre of it all, there was a sinister change. A jagged black hole in space, which seemed to pulse and quiver with evil life.

'A hole in space,' said the Chancellor slowly. 'A no-where, a no-place, a void. According to all known scientific laws, nothing can exist there. Yet somehow, through that hole, vital cosmic energy is draining away despite all we can do to stop it.'

The President checked some readings on a nearby control console. 'The energy loss is worsening, my lord. Soon the Time Travel facility itself will be endangered. Without it we shall be helpless.' He smashed his fist down on the console. 'We are being *consumed*, my lord, by a Force equal yet opposite to our own, from the Universe of Anti-matter. I am sure that this attack on the Doctor is yet another manifestation of that Force.'

The Chancellor led the way back to the screen showing the SOS. 'Ah yes, the Doctor,' he brooded.

'He has asked for our help, and it is our duty to give it. Whatever his errors, he is still a Time Lord.'

'No-one can be spared, my lord. *Everyone*, every scrap of our power, is needed to combat the energy-drain. Unless . . . unless . . . Yes! It's the only way. If your excellency will accompany me?'

With suddenly renewed energy, the President strode to another section of the vast Control Room. Scurrying a little, his dignity forgotten, the Chancellor followed him. The two old men halted before a darkened screen where a Junior Time Lord sat in gloomy idleness. He started, as the President tapped him on the shoulder. 'Show me a section of the Doctor's earlier time stream—*before* he changed his appearance.' Astonished, the young Time Lord, a boy of a mere two hundred years, glanced up at his superior's face. 'Show me!' ordered the President. The young Time Lord's hands flickered over the complex controls before him, and the screen glowed into life. A picture formed, the savage and hostile landscape of some primitive planet. Across it was running a rather small man in eccentric and colourful clothing. From the pace at which he was moving it seemed likely that something very nasty indeed was after him.

The President turned triumphantly to the Chancellor. 'You see, my lord? We cannot help the Doctor, but perhaps he can help himself!'

The Chancellor was appalled. 'I forbid it. You cannot allow him to cross his own time stream and meet his earlier self. The First Time Law expressly forbids—'

The President interrupted him, in itself an unheard-of audacity. He gestured round the almost-empty, darkened hall. 'We are all of us fighting for our lives. Is this a time for rules?'

'You cannot do this!'

The President's voice was firm. 'My lord, I must. I must and I *will*. It is the Doctor's only hope. Ours too, perhaps.'

For a moment the two old men glared at each other. The Junior Time Lord sat like a mouse, scarcely daring to breathe. The Chancellor's eyes fell first. 'Very well. On your own head be it.' Salvaging his dignity as best he could, the Chancellor turned and strode from the hall. The President turned to the quaking young Time Lord and began rapping out instructions. Once again the Junior Time Lord's hands began moving across the controls . . .

The Doctor, Jo and Sergeant Benton gazed gloomily at the TARDIS's scanner screen. It showed the inside of the laboratory, now almost completely bare, the glowing, crackling mass of the jelly thrashing to and fro, unable to complete its mission and engulf the TARDIS itself. From time to time it extruded a tentacle and touched it, drawing back with an angry crackle as it was repelled by the protective force-field. Suddenly the TARDIS vibrated, almost as if it had landed. The Doctor looked suspiciously at his two companions. 'What was that? Nobody touched anything, did they?'

Jo and Benton shook their heads in denial. A round wooden object rolled across the floor and stopped by the Doctor's foot. He picked it up, frowning. 'Some kind of flute! Is it yours, Jo?'

Jo shook her head. The Doctor examined the little instrument curiously.

'The funny thing is, it seems strangely familiar. A flute . . .' The Doctor rubbed his chin, trying to recapture a fugitive trace of memory.

A hand sneaked under his arm and neatly plucked the flute from his fingers. 'Properly speaking,' said a rather huffy voice, 'the instrument is known as a recorder!'

They all whirled round. Standing just behind them was a middle-sized, middle-aged man in a shabby old frock coat and rather baggy check trousers. His untidy black hair hung in a fringe over his forehead, and his dark brown eyes were at once humorous and sad. Jo Grant took to him instantly, and instinctively smiled at him. The stranger smiled back, and gave a little trill on the recorder. He frowned, tried again, and looked accusingly at the Doctor. 'You haven't been trying to *play* it, have you?' The Doctor seemed too astonished to reply. The stranger looked round the TARDIS, and spotted the picture on the scanner screen. He rushed up to it with child-like curiosity. 'Oh dear, oh dear, we are in trouble, aren't we? Just as well I turned up!'

Suddenly he noticed Benton who was looking at him open-mouthed. To Jo's astonishment, Benton said, 'Hullo, Doctor! Where did you spring from?'

The newcomer rushed up to Benton and shook him warmly by the hand. 'Corporal Benton, isn't it? Haven't seen you since that nasty business with the Cybermen. How's the dear old Brigadier?'

Benton tapped his sleeve. 'Actually, it's Sergeant Benton now, Doc. And the Brig's fine.'

'My dear fellow, congratulations.' The strange little man shook Benton's hand again.

Jo sidled up to the Doctor. 'Who is he? Is he one of *Them*?' Jo gazed upwards, with the gesture she instinctively used whenever she referred to the Time Lords.

The Doctor sighed. 'Not exactly, Jo. He's not so much one of Them as one of *me*!'

The stranger came across to Jo, putting a friendly arm across her shoulders. 'Oh no, no, no, it isn't that at all. I hate to seem contrary, but I do feel you should have the *correct* explanation.' He pointed to the tall elegant figure of the Doctor who was glaring down at him in mounting outrage. 'The fact of the matter is,' said the newcomer confidingly, '*he* is one of *me*.'

In a state of total confusion, Jo looked from one to the other of them. 'You mean you're *both* Time Lords?'

The little man patted her on the back. 'Not just both Time Lords, you see. Both the same Time Lord!' He beamed at her triumphantly, as if this made everything clear.

Lifting the stranger's arm from her shoulders, the Doctor drew Jo to his side. 'Please, you're only confusing my assistant. The fact of the matter is, Jo, he is me, and I am him!' Jo buried her head in her hands.

Benton said suddenly, 'Maybe *I* can help, miss. You see, when I first met the Doctor here . . .' Benton pointed to the tall white-haired man at Jo's side, 'he looked like *him*!' He nodded towards the stranger.

Jo struggled to understand. She looked at the little man. 'You mean you're the Doctor as he used to be—before he changed? Then in that case how did you get *here*—and *now*?'

'That's what I'd like to know,' said the Doctor indignantly. 'You've absolutely no right to pop up like this. What about the First Time Law?'

'Oh bother the First Time Law,' said the little man. (In order to avoid confusion, Jo decided to think of him as Doctor Two.) 'Don't you realise this is an emergency? Our fellow Time Lords are under siege, and they've sent me to help you. Your effectiveness is now doubled.'

The Doctor snorted. 'Doubled? Halved, more like it, with you to look after!'

Doctor Two said, 'Now don't be ungracious, old chap. I think the first thing to do is for me to put you in the picture.'

The Doctor opened his mouth to protest, but before he could say anything, Doctor Two reached out and put a hand to his temple with a curiously formal gesture. It was obviously familiar to the Doctor, for he grunted a rather surly, 'Oh all right,' and put his hand to the newcomer's temple in the same way.

'Contact!' said Doctor Two firmly, and the two Time Lords became instantly motionless.

Jo and Benton looked on in astonishment. The two very different figures were standing absolutely still, but you could almost feel the power of the mental energy flowing between them. Suddenly Jo realised what was going on. 'Look,' she whispered to Benton, 'they're having some kind of telepathic conference.'

And that, indeed, was exactly what was happening. In the newcomer's mind was flooding everything that had happened since the arrival of the cosmic-ray research balloon at the bird sanctuary; the vanishing of Hollis, and of Tyler; the sudden attack of the jelly and the creatures it had formed. In return, the Doctor received a full history of the sudden appearance of the black hole in space and of the way it was gradually draining the cosmic energy of the Time Lords, and threatening to disintegrate the fabric of the entire Universe. In a matter of seconds the process was complete and the two Doctors stepped apart, their faces equally grave.

The first, Jo's Doctor, gazed thoughtfully at the scanner screen where the scene in the lab was unchanged. The second Doctor began to tootle on his flute. Jo found the sound rather soothing, but it was soon apparent that the Doctor didn't share her view. He turned angrily to his other self and snapped, 'Must you?'

Doctor Two looked hurt. 'It helps me to think!'

'Well it stops *me* from thinking at all!'

'Are we going to take this attitude to my music the whole time?'

'Quite frankly, yes we are. In a serious situation like this, I've no time to listen to paratiddles on your piccolo!'

In a matter of minutes the two Doctors were arguing furiously. The air of the TARDIS rang with cries of 'Philistine!' and 'Cacophony!' 'Balderdash!' and 'Tripe!'

Jo glanced up at Benton doubtfully. It didn't look as if this strange collaboration was going to work at all.

The same thought was occurring to the Junior Time Lord, who was watching the scene on his monitor. He looked up, as the imposing figure of the President came up to him.

'We've achieved the transference you asked for, my lord President, but I'm afraid it isn't working out too well.'

'And why not?'

The young Time Lord pointed to the gesticulating figures on the screen. 'All they do is quarrel, sir.'

The President thought for a moment. Then he smiled. 'I suppose it's natural enough. Two opposing parts of the same personality. They're too much alike to agree. They need someone to keep them in order. Show me the Doctor's first incarnation.'

The Junior Time Lord swallowed hard. 'Him too, sir? But in view of the attitude of the Chancellor—'

'We've already shattered the First Time Law, my boy. A third Doctor won't make matters very much worse.'

The Time Lord obeyed, making new adjustments to his controls. The scene in the TARDIS faded, and slowly a face appeared on the screen in its place, a lined, white-haired old man with a face full of dignity, power, and a touch of cranky bad temper.

The President smiled. 'Excellent. He'll keep them in order.'

The Junior Time Lord began to check the readings

on his console. 'I don't think I can achieve a full physical manifestation for you, my lord. The energy levels are getting too low now.'

'That isn't needed, my boy. All we need is a presence, something to remind those impetuous youngsters down there of their duty. Do the best you can . . .'

Obediently, the Junior Time Lord bent over his controls.

In the TARDIS, the two Doctors were distracted from their argument when they noticed that the screen of the TARDIS had suddenly gone blank. The new Doctor rushed to the controls, and tried to get the picture back, but with no success. He peered up accusingly at his other self.

'You've been fiddling with it, haven't you?'

'It was perfectly all right until *you* touched it,' said the Doctor rather unfairly. He bustled the newcomer away from the console. 'Now if you'd only leave things to me . . .'

The second Doctor ducked indignantly round him in an attempt to get at the controls. 'Leave things to you? A fine pickle we'd all be in!'

In the heat of their dispute they both ignored the scanner screen. Jo was the first to see a new picture forming, the face of a rather cross-looking white-haired old man. Faintly she said, 'Doctors, look, both of you!'

Both Doctors turned towards the screen. At the sight of the face they seemed literally dumbstruck, as if someone had turned off their voices. The fierce old man on the screen surveyed them for a moment. It was obvious that somehow he could see them—and he wasn't very impressed. 'So you're what I have become, are you? A dandy and a clown!'

Tht two Doctors stood before the screen like guilty schoolboys sent to the headmaster, not daring to reply. The old man sniffed disdainfully. 'Well,' he said sharply, 'what have you done to deal with the problem? Anything? Anything at all?'

It was Doctor Two who plucked up courage to reply. 'We've er, assessed the situation,' he said, a little lamely.

The old man on the screen sniffed again. 'As I thought—nothing. Other than squabble like a couple of spoiled brats, that is.'

The Doctor joined in. 'Well it isn't all that easy, you know.'

The old man cut across him. 'As I said. Nothing.'

'So far we don't even know what that stuff is,' pleaded Doctor Two.

'Don't you? Then I'll tell you. It's a bridge. And what's a bridge for, *eh*?'

Rather to her own surprise Jo suddenly piped up 'Crossing?'

The old man gave a shrill cackle. 'Gel's got more sense than the two of you put together! Exactly, crossing! So stop dilly-dallying, you two. One of you must stay to keep an eye on the situation here, and the other must cross it.' With that his image faded from the screen. Immediately both Doctors started to fiddle with the scanner control, but succeeded only in getting in each other's way.

'There, you've lost him,' said the Doctor accusingly.

'*I* lost him?' said Doctor Two indignantly. 'If you would only leave the working of the TARDIS to someone who understands it . . .'

All at once the two Doctors were squabbling again. There came a sudden parade-ground roar from Sergeant Benton. 'Oy, you two! Pack that up!'

Amazed, both Doctors fell silent. Taking advantage of the lull, Jo asked, 'Who *was* that?' She nodded towards the screen, now once more showing the blob of jelly waiting in the laboratory outside.

Both Doctors answered her at once. 'Us!'

'Well,' said Jo sternly, 'I think you ought to listen to what he said, and stop being childish.'

For a moment both Doctors glared at her. Then the mouth of the newer, smaller one twitched into a reluctant grin. He looked up at his other self. 'She's quite right, you know.'

The taller Doctor cleared his throat. 'Harrumph! Well, I hope that nothing I said about your music gave offence. Rather a catchy little tune, actually.'

'My dear fellow, think nothing of it. My fault entirely.'

Their mutual apologies completed, the two Doctors beamed affectionately at each other. Their faces became serious again as they looked at the scanner screen. Doctor Two fished in the pocket of his battered old coat and produced a large silver coin. 'Will you call?'

He spun the coin high in the air.

'Heads!' said the Doctor.

Doctor Two caught the coin on the back of one hand, slapping the palm of the other down on top of it. He lifted his hand and looked at the coin. 'Bad luck, old chap,' he said hastily, and the coin disappeared into his pocket before the Doctor could look at it.

The Doctor threw him a suspicious look. 'Right! If you'll be ready to disconnect the force-field?'

Jo and Sergeant Benton had been standing ignored in the background.

'Hey, just a minute,' protested Benton. 'What are you two up to?'

The Doctors continued to ignore him. Doctor Two went to the controls and switched off the force-field. He touched another control, and the TARDIS door swung open. Calmly the Doctor stepped out into the laboratory. Doctor Two touched the control to close the door.

With a shock of horror Jo suddenly realised what 'crossing the bridge' meant.

The Doctor was going to deliver himself up to the jelly and see where it took him. Before anyone could stop her, she leaped through the already-closing TARDIS door and tried to pull the Doctor back.

The Tardis door swung to behind her.

The Doctor called, 'Jo, get back inside!' But the door was already closed. Jo ran to the Doctor's arms for shelter as, crackling greedily, the huge, shimmering mound of jelly rolled towards them.

On the TARDIS screen, Benton and the second Doctor watched helplessly. The mound of jelly rolled over Jo and the Doctor. As it touched them there came a brilliant, soundless flash and Jo and the Doctor vanished.

4

Beyond the Unknown

Sergeant Benton made an instinctive move to dash out of the TARDIS. But the new Doctor, or as far as Benton was concerned, the old Doctor, Jo's Doctor Two, laid a restraining hand on his arm.

'Steady on, Sergeant, they're out of our reach now. He knew what he was doing—at least, I hope he did.'

'Will they be all right, Doctor?'

The little man reached up and patted Benton reassuringly on the shoulder. 'As far as I can tell, that stuff out there has gone to a great deal of trouble to get me—or rather, him—, and I doubt if whoever or whatever sent it simply wanted us dead. No, they've both been transported somewhere.'

'I *saw* that—the question is, where?'

Doctor Two shrugged. 'Where indeed?' Suddenly he darted over to the scanner and peered at it. 'Do you know, I think our blobby friend out there has just gone off the boil.'

Benton looked over his shoulder. The blob of jelly, now shrunken and still, lay quietly in one corner of the laboratory, showing no sign of its former ferocity. 'Right, let's get some explosives and blow it to smithereens,' said Benton eagerly.

'I think we can be a bit more subtle than that,

Sergeant. We must study it. It may still have a great deal to tell us.' He opened the door of the TARDIS, and they both came slowly out into the laboratory. Cautiously they approached the jelly-blob. It stirred and crackled, but only very faintly.

The door opened and the Brigadier, revolver in hand, peered cautiously round it. At the sight of two figures bending over to look at the blob he snapped, 'For Heaven's sake be careful of that stuff.'

At the sound of his voice, Sergeant Benton straightened up and turned round. So did the second Doctor.

When he saw him the Brigadier opened his mouth like a stranded fish, spluttering to get the words out. 'Oh no!' he gasped finally.

Doctor Two beamed at him. 'Oh yes, Brigadier. How are you, my dear fellow?'

'Pretty well, thanks,' said the Brigadier, returning the handshake automatically. Then realising that he was greeting a man who too all intents and purposes no longer existed, he spluttered, 'What the blazes is going on here?'

'It's him, sir,' explained Benton rather obviously. 'The one we met first of all.'

'I can see that. Why has he changed back again?'

'He hasn't, sir, not exactly. This one just sort of popped up. There are two of them now! There was even a third—but he was only on the scanner screen.'

'Heaven preserve us!' said the Brigadier faintly. He looked for a stool to sit on, but by now they had all disappeared. He leaned against the wall and spoke in a voice of unnatural calm, 'Sergeant Benton! Will you please tell me exactly what's been going on?'

Benton did his best. When he'd stumbled to the end of his long, complicated and confused story, the second Doctor said cheerfully :

'There you are, Brigadier. All perfectly simple really.'

'I'm sorry,' said the Brigadier crisply, 'but I don't believe a word of it. It's perfectly obvious what's happened. You've been fiddling with that infernal machine of yours. Somehow or other you've changed your appearance back, and shot poor Miss Grant off heaven knows where.'

Doctor Two sighed. 'Believe what you like, Brigadier, as long as it makes you happy.'

The Brigadier straightened up. Now he'd found an explanation that satisfied *him*, he was his old self again. 'I want two things from you, Doctor. An effective way of controlling that jelly stuff, and the return of Miss Grant safe and sound.'

Doctor Two sighed. 'I'll do my best for you. But I can't promise anything. Wherever they are, Miss Grant and my other self, we can't contact them. That's the trouble with anti-matter. You can see the effect, but never the cause.' He gave his sudden beaming smile. 'Like a punch on the nose from the invisible man!'

The Brigadier waved his revolver at the blob, which still lay inertly in its corner. 'Then what is this stuff?'

'That's anti-matter. The invisible man!'

The Brigadier felt his head begin to spin. 'But I thought matter and anti-matter couldn't meet—not without a colossal explosion.'

'That's right. I'm afraid it means that whoever

created this stuff, and sent it here, is a good deal cleverer than we are.'

'Is there *anything* you can do, Doctor?'

'I can study it. Try to learn some of its secrets. But first I must make sure it stays harmless.'

'And how do you propose to do that?'

Doctor Two rubbed his hands. 'I shall confuse it,' he announced happily. 'Feed it useless and conflicting information.'

He wandered round the laboratory, and suddenly flung open the door of the Doctor's electronic spares cupboard. It had escaped being 'vanished', perhaps because it was 'built-in', flush to the wall. He examined the loaded shelves with evident delight. Pulling out piece after piece of electronic equipment, he gathered all he could carry and sat down cross-legged on the floor. Benton looked on admiringly as a complicated lash-up of equipment started taking shape beneath the second Doctor's hands.

'Pass me that induction coil, will you, Sergeant? Oh, and I'd better have one of those booster circuits.'

Hurriedly Benton obeyed, adding to the pile of equipment on the floor.

The Brigadier looked at the pair of them. They looked like a couple of kids playing with a train-set. Deciding that there was nothing useful he could say or do, he turned and marched out of the laboratory.

Benton and Doctor Two didn't even notice him go.

*   *   *   *   *

Jo Grant could never really decide what had actually happened to her. The moment the rolling mass of the

45

jelly-blob touched them, the silent flash blinded her eyes. She seemed to feel that the real world was dissolving around her. She had a sensation, surely an illusion, of leaving the earth altogether, of rushing headlong through space towards a patch of deep impenetrable blackness, a kind of black hole. . . . The hole came nearer and nearer, and as it swallowed her up, she lost consciousness.

She came to, much, much later it seemed, at the sound of the Doctor's voice. 'Jo! Come on, wake up. Jo—can you hear me?' Slowly she opened her eyes, and to her enormous relief saw the Doctor looking down at her. She managed a nod, and a weak smile. If the Doctor was with her, things couldn't be so bad after all. He helped her to sit up, and she looked around. Stretching as far as she could see was a sort of plain of dunes, dull grey in colour, bleak, desolate and lifeless. The sky was a threatening purple, and everything about the place seemed somehow horribly wrong. Jo realised that it was completely and utterly silent. No wind-noise, no bird-song—just a dead, sinister calm.

She struggled to her feet, shivering. 'Doctor, where are we? Why is everything so strange?' A new terror struck her. Wasn't there a place called Limbo, a featureless nowhere between Heaven and Hell? 'Doctor, we're not—dead, are we?'

The Doctor's familiar laugh broke the deadly silence like a breath of normality. 'Not a bit of it! This is a place. A singularly unpleasant place, but a place all the same. And we've been brought here. Let's take a look around, shall we?'

The two lonely figures started trudging across the featureless grey landscape. They climbed a grey dune and looked around. Before them stretched an endless sea of more dunes, more hollows.

Suddenly Jo pointed. 'Doctor, look!' Standing incongruously in the next hollow was a green painted filing cabinet. 'That's ours,' said Jo almost indignantly. 'It used to be in the laboratory.'

The Doctor nodded. 'So it did. But then, so did we! It was brought here, exactly as we were.'

They trudged on. Soon they came across more odds and ends of UNIT furniture, a laboratory bench, stools, even a hat-stand, all dotted at random around the grey dunes. The Doctor climbed another dune and gave a yell of delight. 'Jo, come and see!' Jo ran up to join him. There in the hollow beneath them was 'Bessie', sedately parked as if ready for a day's outing. They ran towards her. Somehow the sight of the little car was immensely cheering. The Doctor gave it a pat on the bonnet. 'You see, Jo? We've been transported like "Bessie" and all that other stuff. Now all we have to do is find out where Here is, and Who brought us.'

Jo climbed into the passenger seat. 'Come along then, Doctor. No point in walking if we don't have to.'

The Doctor looked at her dubiously. 'Use "Bessie"? Well, we can try. I'm not sure if mechanical laws apply in a place like this.' He pressed the starter, and the engine turned over immediately. The Doctor grinned. 'Bless my soul!' He turned to Jo and said in a chauffeur's voice, 'Where to, miss?'

Jo smiled, and waved airily. 'Just drive around, my good man!'

And drive around they did. 'Bessie' climbed valiantly up the low hills, and lurched down into the hollows. It was better riding than walking, but they soon began to feel that they weren't achieving much. Since everywhere was so exactly the same, there seemed little point in moving at all. The Doctor halted the car on top of one of the higher dunes. Jo stood up and looked around. The view in every direction was exactly the same. 'Oh what's the use,' she sighed. 'We could wander round here for ever—there's nothing to see.'

'Oh yes there is,' said the Doctor suddenly. 'Look!' He pointed. Halfway up the side of one of the dunes a line of footprints began. They led over the top of the dune and out of sight. The Doctor climbed out of the car. 'Come on, Jo. We'll follow them on foot. Better get a look at whatever it is before it sees us.'

They followed the trail of the footprints up the dune down the other side, and then over the next dune. Suddenly the Doctor stopped. 'Listen, Jo.' From the other side of the dune was coming a low, obsessive muttering. The Doctor motioned Jo onwards and they followed the footsteps towards the source of the sound. As they came closer, Jo could hear what the voice was saying. It was talking to itself in a quiet, reasonable tone.

'$E = MC^2$. I mean, there's no doubt about *that*, is there? But if you equate gravitation with acceleration, I must have travelled here faster than light. And that's impossible, by definition.'

Jo and the Doctor peered over the top of the dune. Stretching ahead of them was a sea, a dull grey sea that was hard to distinguish from the land. And sitting cross-legged on the shore, idly tossing pebbles into the water, was a short sturdy figure, talking to himself in a steady, reasonable monotone.

It was Doctor Tyler, the man who had started the whole thing when he brought them his orange-coloured box.

Excitedly Jo called, 'Doctor Tyler!' and ran towards him, the Doctor following close behind.

Tyler was almost pathetically glad to see them. Words poured out of him in a flood. 'It's Miss Grant, isn't it—and the Doctor? How did you get here? Same as me, I suppose. I was in your lab, and I'd just developed that plate, then—bingo! Fascinating place this. Lonely though. And quiet! I've been talking to myself, just to hear a human voice. I don't suppose you know where we are, Doctor?' he ended hopefully.

The Doctor rubbed his chin. 'Well, only in a general way. We're at the other end of your streak of space-lightning, transported through a black hole. We're in a stable world in a Universe of anti-matter. An anomaly within an impossibility.'

'Oh yes?' said Jo faintly.

Tyler grinned. 'What the Doctor means is that a place like this shouldn't exist in a cosmos like this, and even if it does, we shouldn't be here anyway. Right, Doctor?'

'Well—something like that. But we are here. Kidnapped—and marooned.'

Tyler nodded, his face grave. 'Aye—and who by, that's what I want to know.' He looked round cautiously. 'There's *things* here, you know, Creatures.'

Instinctively Jo drew closer to the Doctor. 'What kind of—things?' she asked nervously.

Tyler drew a deep breath. 'Well, they're man-shaped. In a nasty, blobby sort of way, that is. Made of some sort of jelly stuff. I've seen 'em moving about. Managed to dodge 'em so far though. They seem to be searching.'

Jo tugged at the Doctor's sleeve. 'Those things that attacked UNIT . . .'

The Doctor nodded. 'We've encountered them too, Doctor Tyler. They seem to be servants of whoever's behind all this. They were searching, you say? Probably for us!'

'I think they've found us, Doctor,' said Jo.

The Doctor and Tyler looked up. The dunes above them were lined with the blobby figures, motionless and waiting. Instinctively the Doctor shouted, 'Run, all of you!'

Before they could move, one of the figures raised a shapeless hand, and the ground exploded at their feet. They ran the other way, and more explosions sprang up to bar their path. Soon they were held, trapped, in a circle of flames. They stood helplessly, waiting, as the hideous, shapeless creatures shambled closer.

*   *   *   *   *

Once again the President and the Chancellor stood in the Temporal Control Room, watching the screen which showed the picture of the black hole in space. It seemed larger, deeper now, as if preparing to swallow up the whole of the Universe.

The President said, 'It grows more powerful moment by moment. It swallows up all the energy we can send against it, draining away our very life.'

The Chancellor returned to his grievance. 'Yet you still waste the little power that remains to us with this ridiculous operation of yours concerning the Doctor. Not only that, you transgress the First Law of Time.'

The President sighed. Still this niggling insistence on rules, while everything was crashing around them.

'In such an emergency, my lord Chancellor,' he began.

'*No* emergency can justify such transgression. The operation must cease.'

In tones equally determined the President countered, 'The operation must continue. It is now our only hope. We can do nothing for ourselves but hold off the disaster a very little longer. The Doctor has gone to the source of the evil. Perhaps there he can . . .'

'The source?' interrupted the Chancellor sharply. 'How is that possible? What is the Doctor's current situation?'

The President smiled wryly. 'It depends which Doctor you mean. The earliest incarnation, the oldest can do no more than advise. The power was too low for a full incarnation. The second is still on Earth, assisting with the situation there.'

'And the third?'

'He has allowed himself to be transported *through* the black hole, to fight the evil at its source.'

The Chancellor looked at the screen again, at the gaping black mouth that threatened to swallow the stars. He turned back to the President, a gleam of triumph in his eyes. 'He has gone—there? Through the black hole? Beyond the Absolute Event horizon, where the laws of science no longer apply?'

Grimly the President nodded.

The Chancellor said, 'Then your rash experiment has already failed. The Doctor is dead!'

5

A Shock for the Brigadier

Doctor Two carefully adjusted the last of a series of reflectors and focused it on the blob. It was now ringed by a circle of reflectors, each one connected to the amazing conglomeration of electronic equipment the Doctor had assembled. It was obviously some kind of force-field generator, thought Benton, though how it worked, and what it did, he couldn't begin to guess. Doctor Two plugged the whole thing into one of the special heavy-duty wall-plugs, and threw a switch. Immediately, fierce blue electric sparks leaped between all the generators. The blob was literally ringed with fire. It thrashed wildly for a moment, and extruded a tentacle. As it touched one of the sparks, the tentacle whipped back, and the blob crackled, almost with a note of pain.

'Sorry, old chap,' said Doctor Two seriously, 'but we can't have you wandering about.'

Benton felt no such sympathy. 'Can't you step up the power, Doctor? Fry the wretched stuff once and for all?'

'Certainly not. What would we learn from that?'

Benton privately thought they might not learn much but he for one would feel a good deal safer.

The Brigadier came in and looked at the Doctor's work approvingly.

'Got it pinned down, eh, Doctor? Well done. I've another little job for you now.'

Doctor Two looked at him suspiciously. 'Oh yes?'

'Chap from the Government has turned up. Wants a full explanation of what's been going on.' The Brigadier coughed. 'I'm leaving it all to you.'

'All right. But won't he think it strange—seeing me, I mean?'

'I've explained all that. You're the Doctor's assistant.'

The second Doctor drew himself up to his full height, such as it was, and said indignantly, 'Now see here, Brigadier . . .'

The Brigadier held up his hand. 'No use fussing, Doctor. The truth would be too much for him. Assistant it will have to be.' He held open the door. 'Come along now.'

Doctor Two hovered indecisively. 'But I've just set up my apparatus. I'll be able to confuse the stuff now.'

'No doubt,' remarked the Brigadier drily. 'Confusion seems to be your forte. But that will have to wait. You're sure that stuff's safe now?'

'Oh yes. We've got it thoroughly tamed, haven't we, Sergeant?'

Benton nodded, a little dubiously. The Brigadier turned to him, 'In that case you'd better stay here and keep an eye on it, Benton.'

Benton nodded, resignedly. 'Yes, sir.' He'd expected something like that.

The second Doctor pressed a remote-control dial into Benton's reluctant hand. 'You'll need this, old chap. You see, it's graded, 0 to 100.' Doctor Two turned a little dial, and Benton saw the figures on the indicator change from 50 to 51, 52 . . . 'O would set the thing free—100 would destroy it. Keep the setting in the middle range and you'll be all right.'

The Brigadier bustled the second Doctor out of the laboratory, and Benton was left alone with the blob. He had developed an almost personal hatred for it and he walked round it, surveying it dubiously. It had reverted to its original size, about that of a large football. It heaved and quivered and crackled faintly. Benton couldn't rid himself of the feeling that it was watching him, waiting its chance. He glared at it threateningly and said seriously, 'Just you watch it, mate. If you so much as twitch at me, you'll get the works.'

The blob seemed to quiver and pulsate with rage. It gave an angry crackle, as if in reply to his threat. 'Right,' said Benton sternly, and turned up the dial on the remote-control unit. 53, 54, 55 . . . The blob quivered even more fiercely. To Benton's horror it started to *grow*. In a matter of minutes, it had doubled in size. Benton twisted the dial frantically, sending the reading up into the 60s, 70s, 80s, 90s . . . Fierce blue sparks from the reflectors blazed all round the blob, but they seemed only to encourage it. It grew larger still. Now the dial was at 100, and still the thing grew. It crashed its way free of the reflectors and lurched towards Benton. He retreated into a corner yelling, 'Doctor, Brigadier, come back.'

The Doctor, who was having a very unsatisfactory conversation with a sceptical Government V.I.P. in the

Brigadier's office, heard the shouts and ran straight out of the room. With a look of mute apology, the Brigadier followed. The V.I.P. was extremely indignant, and decided to turn in an unfavourable report on the Brigadier as soon as possible.

When Doctor Two ran into the laboratory, the Brigadier close behind him, the jelly-blob had Benton cornered, and was stretching out a menacing tentacle. As soon as the second Doctor entered it turned away from Benton and started menacing *him*. Cautiously he backed away. The blob pursued him, hissing and crackling.

Benton seized his chance, ducked out of his corner, and slipped past the blob to join the others. All three made for the door, but the blob anticipated their move, flowing swiftly across the doorway to cut off their retreat.

His eyes fixed on the blob, Doctor Two edged towards the TARDIS. He produced his key and quickly opened the door. 'Inside, both of you!'

'Oh no, you don't get me in your box of tricks,' said the Brigadier firmly. Not bothering to argue, Doctor Two grabbed him, and with a show of surprising strength virtually threw him inside. Benton followed and the Doctor ducked inside the TARDIS just as the jelly lashed out menacingly.

He shot across to the console, closed the door and muttering 'Force-field, force-field, force-field,' started the TARDIS ticking over. Then he collapsed against the console with a sigh of relief. (So frantically had he been rushing to get the force-field working, that he failed to notice when his beloved flute dropped from the top pocket of his coat, rolled across the console, and dropped somewhere inside the inner workings of the TARDIS.)

Doctor Two switched on the scanner, and he and Benton watched the blob, now swollen to such an enormous size that it almost filled the laboratory. 'I did what you said, Doc,' Benton said reproachfully. 'But it only made the thing worse. Seemed to make it stronger, not weaker.'

The Doctor wrinkled his brow and scratched his head. Suddenly he slapped his brow in a gesture of despair. 'Of course! We were dealing with anti-matter. All my calculations should have been reversed. We weren't calming it—we were stimulating it!'

The Brigadier was staring around him with an air of polite interest. 'Do you know, Doctor,' he said suddenly, 'this thing seems to be bigger on the inside than on the outside?'

'Well, I had noticed. You see it's dimensionally transcendental and—'

'Never mind your scientific mumbo jumbo, Doctor. Some kind of optical illusion,' the Brigadier said shrewdly. 'All done with mirrors, I dare say.'

The Doctor was searching his pockets. 'You haven't seen my flute anywhere, have you?'

'What are you talking about, Doctor?'

'My flute—wooden thing about so long, with holes in it.'

'Never mind your wretched flute. Let me out of this contraption.'

'I'm afraid I can't do that. You'd never make it across the room.'

He pointed to the scanner screen. The entire laboratory was filled with a vast pulsating mass of jelly, which was beginning to flow out into the corridors.

The Brigadier was frantic. 'Doctor, you've got to let me out. I must warn the men.'

Doctor Two shook his head. 'I'm sorry, it's impossible.'

Benton produced his walkie-talkie. 'Why don't you call them up on this, sir?'

Somewhat annoyed that he hadn't thought of this himself, the Brigadier took the set from Benton and snapped, 'This is the Brigadier. Does anyone read me?'

There came an answering crackle and a voice said, 'Communications room here, sir. Corporal Palmer. Where are you, sir?' There was a note of panic in the voice as it went on, 'Sir, that jelly stuff's on the move again. It seems to be filling the entire building. What do we do?'

'Evacuate,' ordered the Brigadier. 'Everybody outside, a safe distance from the building. Form up on the hill, and wait further instructions. Brigadier out. Oh, just a minute.'

'Sir?'

'See that chap from Whitehall gets away safely, will you? Make my apologies and tell him our appointment will have to be unavoidably postponed.' The Brigadier switched off the walkie-talkie. 'Well, Doctor, what next?'

The Doctor was still fishing round in his many pockets. 'We sit, and wait and think, I'm afraid. Would you care for a gobstopper?'

He produced a grimy paper bag, offered it to the

Brigadier (who rejected it rather irritably) and said, 'I wish I could find my flute. I think best to music.'

Benton, who was still watching the scanner screen, said, 'Doctor, the picture's changing. It's that old bloke again.'

Doctor Two rushed to the screen and saw the features of his first incarnation glaring at him disapprovingly. 'Well,' said the sharp old voice, 'made any progress?'

Doctor Two sighed, and decided to own up. After all if you can't be honest with yourself . . . 'No,' he said firmly. 'None whatsoever. How are our fellow Time Lords?'

'Getting steadily weaker. They can't seem to check the energy loss.'

'Is there anything I can do to help? I'd welcome your advice.'

'Turn off the TARDIS force-field.'

Doctor Two looked horrified. 'But that would mean—'

'Well of course it would,' interrupted the old Doctor querulously. 'But I'm afraid it may be the only way. Surely you can see that? Use our intelligence!' And with that, the lined old face faded away. The rampaging jelly-blob filled the scanner once again.

The second Doctor stood slumped by the scanner, his face grave and resigned. Benton said, 'You're not going to do it, are you, Doctor—turn off the force-field?'

'Oh yes, I think so.' He nodded towards the scanner. '*He* told me to. And I've always had great respect for his advice.'

The Brigadier looked at him in perplexity. 'Am I correct in thinking, Doctor, that if you cut off the force-field, that stuff out there can get at the TARDIS?'

Doctor Two said cheerfully, 'Absolutely correct. Hold on, everyone!' Before they could stop him, he reached out and switched off the force-field.

Immediately a series of tremendous jolts started to shake the TARDIS, sending it lurching from side to side. There was a final tremendous jolt, and the TARDIS seemed to spin in mid-air, throwing its occupants about like dice inside a shaker. They crashed against walls, floors and ceiling, and everything went black.

Corporal Palmer had received the Brigadier's order to evacuate with the greatest relief. He lost no time in carrying it out. For the second time that day the UNIT H.Q. staff poured out of the building at top speed, forming up on the overlooking hill. A very angry Whitehall V.I.P. had been whizzed back to London in his limousine, and now Palmer and the rest of the UNIT troops were watching the main building, wondering what would happen next. Palmer thought he was prepared for anything. But he was wrong. The jelly-like substance, now swollen to fantastic volume, could be seen pouring through the empty building. Empty that is, except for those trapped inside the TARDIS. Soon every room in the building was filled with the heaving, crackling mass. The stuff was even rising outside the outer walls, until the outlines of the entire building were obscured by the glistening blob.

Palmer made another attempt to get through on his walkie-talkie. 'Brigadier, this is Corporal Palmer. The evacuation is now complete. Are you still all right? Shall we mount a rescue attempt?'

There was no reply. Suddenly an enormous white flash filled the air. Palmer dropped his walkie-talkie and, like the rest of the UNIT troops, covered his eyes with his hands. For one terrible moment, he thought they had all been blinded. He opened his eyes and saw—blackness. Then to his infinite relief, the blackness gave way to a kind of red mist. This too faded and restored more or less normal vision, though everything seemed very blurred. Blinking his eyes, Palmer looked at UNIT H.Q. It was gone.

He rubbed his streaming eyes with his fists and looked again. The entire building had disappeared. Even the foundations were gone. All that was left was a huge rectangular patch of black earth where the building had once stood. Unbelievingly, Palmer stumbled towards it.

*   *   *   *   *

Inside the TARDIS it was Doctor Two who recovered consciousness first. He found himself slumped over the top of the control console. He slid down, groaning a little from aches and stiffness, and felt himself rapidly all over, concluding with relief that although most of him was bruised, nothing was actually broken. He thought that it was probably the shock of transportation, rather than the banging about, which had knocked them all out.

Sergeant Benton was sprawled in a heap on the base of the console, the Brigadier slumped face down near the door. The Doctor looked at them sadly, wondering how to break the news. The first thing, he decided, was to wake them up.

A few minutes later, the Brigadier and Sergeant Benton were both on their feet, stretching and groaning, and gazing around in confusion. The Doctor checked them over and decided that, like himself, they were more shaken up than actually damaged.

As soon as he was fully conscious, the Brigadier's first thought was for the safety of his men. He snatched up the walkie-talkie, which was lying in a corner, and flicked the control. 'Corporal Palmer, do you read me? Palmer, what's the situation out there?' The set crackled, but there was no reply. The Brigadier shook it irritably. 'Must have been damaged in the explosion.'

Doctor Two looked at him sadly. 'I'm afraid you won't get through on that thing, Brigadier. It hasn't quite got the range. And that wasn't an explosion—not in the way you mean.'

'Nonsense. I know blast-effect when I feel it. That jelly stuff must have blown itself up. Maybe that contraption of yours did the job after all, Doctor. Switch on that scanner thing.'

Silently Doctor Two obeyed. The scanner showed an empty laboratory, with no sign of the blob. 'There you are,' said the Brigadier triumphantly. 'We've got rid of it.'

'On the contrary, Brigadier, it's got rid of us.'

The Brigadier ignored him. 'Open the doors now please. I'll just pop outside and see what's going on.'

'I really don't advise it.'

'Come now, Doctor, we can't stay inside here for ever.'

'No, I suppose we can't. Very well, I'll open the doors. But I think you should prepare yourself for a bit of a shock.'

He operated the control, the TARDIS door opened and the Brigadier marched purposefully out.

Doctor Two called after him, 'Brigadier, wait . . .' But the Brigadier was gone. He sighed, 'Oh dear, oh dear, I do wish he'd listen. Come along, Sergeant Benton, we'd better get after him.'

They followed into the laboratory, but the impatient Brigadier had already moved on. Doctor Two looked around almost admiringly. 'Most ingenious. I suppose the stuff found the TARDIS a bit indigestible by itself, so it swallowed some of the surrounding matter as well. Like washing down a pill with a swig of water.'

'What are you on about, Doc?' said Benton suspiciously. 'Are you trying to tell me the whole place has moved?'

'That's right.'

'Where are we then?'

Doctor Two nodded towards the direction taken by the departed Brigadier. 'Not where *he* thinks we are.'

The Brigadier marched along the empty, silent corridors, pleased to see that the evacuation had been carried out as ordered. Curious how quiet everything was. He was on his way to the front door. From there he would be able to see Corporal Palmer on the hill, signal they were all safe. The Brigadier reached the main door and flung it open. He opened his mouth to call, but no sound came out.

There was no green hill, no Corporal Palmer, no UNIT troops to be seen. No roads, no buildings, no fields, no trees. Just miles of grey dunes, stretching ahead as far as the eye could see.

6

In the Hands of the Enemy

Herded by the circle of blobby figures, the Doctor, Jo and Tyler trudged wearily across the endless grey landscape. Their guards herded them like sheep-dogs. If they strayed from the right path, the ground erupted in flame before their feet. There was never any doubt as to which way they were intended to go.

Jo was almost dropping with weariness. She felt as if the nightmare journey had gone on forever. The ghastly sameness of the featureless dunes meant that they didn't even *feel* they were getting anywhere. It was like walking endlessly on the spot in some terrible dream. Jo stumbled, and held the Doctor's arm for support. 'I can't keep this up much longer, Doctor.'

Gently he steadied her on her feet. 'You won't have to. I think we've reached our destination.'

For quite some time, Jo simply hadn't bothered to look around her. Since there was nothing to see, she'd simply watched her own feet stumbling through the grey sand. Wearily she lifted her head and followed the direction of the Doctor's pointing finger. She gave a gasp of surprise.

In front of them the grey desert had levelled out, and there, in the middle distance, stood a towering castle. It seemed to have been beaten from solid brass. Hundreds of towers and slender minarets glinted dully beneath the lowering purple sky, giving the whole place a look of oriental opulence, like the Arabian Nights castle of some Caliph. The massive main gates were open. Inside they could see only blackness.

Jo clutched the Doctor's arm. 'We haven't got to go in there, have we?'

The Doctor took a step to one side, and a burst of flame sent him back on the road to the castle. 'I'm afraid there's no alternative,' he said gently. 'And it would be very rude to keep our host waiting.'

Tyler looked up at the gleaming, sinister castle. 'Whoever he is, I don't reckon much to his taste in architecture,' he grunted. Soon all three of them were trudging through the massive brazen gates into the darkness of the castle beyond.

They found themselves in a vast shadowy hall. On every side parabolic arches stretched up to the impossibly distant ceiling. With a clang that made Jo jump, the gates swung to behind them.

'What now?' whispered Tyler.

The Doctor spoke in his normal voice. 'I've no idea,' he said. 'I expect someone will let us know.'

'GREETINGS!'

The single word, spoken in a deep resonant voice, echoed and resounded around the hall. They looked towards the source. At the end of the hall, framed in a patch of brilliant light (like a Superstar in a spotlight, thought Jo irreverently), stood a huge, imposing figure. It was a good seven feet tall, and it wore long metallic robes that reflected the gleaming bronze of the walls. It was crowned with a terrifying brazen mask, a huge, cruel metal face with long slanting eye-slits. With a shudder of horror, Jo saw that behind the eye-slits there was—nothing. Only blackness.

'Our host, I presume,' murmured the Doctor and began walking towards the patch of light. Reluctantly, the others followed.

The Doctor gazed up at the terrifying figure, made larger still by the raised metal dais on which it stood. 'Who are you?' he asked boldly. 'Why did you bring us here?'

There was a moment's pause, then the great booming voice spoke again. 'My purpose will soon be revealed to you, Time Lord. As for my name in the legends of our people, I am known as Omega.' The clanging syllables of the name ran round the great brazen hall, until their echoes died away in the high vaulted ceiling.

Jo looked up at the Doctor. It was all too obvious that the name meant a great deal to him. She had never seen him look so shocked. In an awe-stricken voice he gasped, 'No—no you can't be. You were destroyed.'

'No, Doctor, as you see, I was *not* destroyed.' A note of strangely incongruous self-pity came into the great voice. 'I have been wronged, Doctor, grievously wronged. Now is the time for my vengeance.'

At a wave of Omega's hand, blob-men appeared from the darkness and began to herd Jo and Tyler away. The Doctor called, 'My friends must not be harmed, Omega. They are here by chance.'

'Do not fear, Doctor.' With a rather sinister emphasis, Omega added, '*They* have no part in my coming vengeance.'

Jo and Tyler were driven down a long gloomy corridor. Their guard paused by a sort of arched recess, and motioned them in. Once they were inside, it moved away into the darkness. Tyler looked round puzzled. 'How do they expect to keep us here, in a cell with no door?'

His question was soon answered. The air at the mouth of the arch shimmered and another wall appeared, blocking it off. Jo drew a deep breath. 'How about that, then?'

'Aye, he's got a few tricks up his sleeves,' agreed Tyler. 'Whoever he is.'

Jo was still thinking about their encounter with Omega. 'The Doctor seemed to know him.'

Tyler grunted. 'Happened he did. Hasn't done us much good though, has it? We're shut up in here, while the Doctor has a nice cosy chat with his old friend.'

'I didn't get the feeling they were *friends*. More like deadly enemies.' Folding her arms, she leaned against the bare metal walls of the cell and shivered. One thought was filling her mind. It was the first time she had ever seen the Doctor afraid.

The Doctor was still afraid, as anyone may be who finds himself face to face with a legend. But he managed to control his fear, keeping his voice steady and his manner calm. Once Jo and Tyler had been taken off, Omega had motioned the Doctor to follow him. Now they were standing in some kind of inner chamber, just behind the great hall. There was still the same richly ornate metallic décor, but one complete wall was occupied by an enormous screen showing a great sweep of space, crowded with a sort of faint starry mist. The Doctor knew he was looking at the Veil Nebula, an enormous mass of gases and cosmic dust. Omega gestured towards it. 'Without me, there would *be* no Time Travel. You and your fellow Time Lords would still be locked into your own Time, as puny as the creatures you so graciously protect.'

The Doctor was all too aware that everything Omega claimed was true. Lamely he said, 'You must have known that your mission was dangerous.'

'Dangerous, yes. Yet I completed it. And I did not expect to be abandoned.'

'You were not abandoned, Omega,' said the Doctor desperately.

The great booming voice overbore him. Again Omega gestured towards the Nebula. 'Once all this was a star, a sun with planets, until *I* arranged its detonation.'

'You were the first of our Solar Engineers. It was your duty...'

'It was my honour. I was to be the one to find and create the power source to give my people mastery over Time itself.'

'And so you did. You succeeded and you were honoured for it.'

'Honoured? I was abandoned. I was the sacrifice to that supernova. Blown out of existence into this world of anti-matter. My brothers became Time Lords, and I was abandoned to my fate, forgotten...' Once more the great voice was steeped in self-pity.

'You were *not* forgotten,' contradicted the Doctor firmly. 'All my life I have known of you, honoured you as the greatest of our heroes. Now you have turned against your own people, you talk of revenge . . .'

Omega made a sweeping gesture, and the picture disappeared from the screen. 'And why not? A hero?' This time the voice was full of bitter scorn. 'I should have been a god!'

Omega turned and strode away. The Doctor followed him, his mind a whirlpool of emotions. On one level, he was still reeling from the shock of realising that the long-dead Omega, the great Solar Engineer who had sacrificed his life to bring the secret of Time Travel to his people, was somehow still alive in this impossible place. But at the forefront of his mind was another terrifying thought. One thing was quite certain. Brooding on his wrongs for untold years had sent Omega mad. Yet in this world he was all powerful. And the Doctor and his friends were in Omega's hands. For the first time in his life, the Doctor knew the full meaning of despair.

He followed Omega into the great hall. For the moment Omega's rage had subsided, and the great figure was wrapped in a brooding silence.

The Doctor said, 'Theoretically, of course, you, this place, that substance of yours—well, it's all impossible.'

'Here, Doctor, *everything* is possible—as you will discover.'

'How did you manage to survive?'

'How does anyone survive? By the force of my will!'

'And the organism you sent to bring us here?'

'I created it from the raw stuff of matter. It has

transformed you, so that you too can exist in this world.'

With complete sincerity, the Doctor said, 'It's all enormously impressive. With all these powers, why do you need help from me?'

'There are some things even I cannot do alone. At this point in my plans, I need the help of a *brother* Time Lord.' There was a wealth of scorn in Omega's voice as he pronounced the last few words.

'I see. And since I was isolated on Earth, you turned your attack to me.'

Omega waved a dismissive hand. 'It amused me —to use you against them.'

'Even if I give you my help, do you really think you can succeed in defeating the other Time Lords—all of them?'

Omega's laugh echoed round the hall. 'But I *am* defeating them. With the forces at my command, I created the black hole. It is draining cosmic energy from their universe into mine. As they grow weaker, I grow stronger.'

'And if I don't co-operate?'

The room darkened. Streaks of jagged light flashed like lightning across the darkness of the roof. The metal walls glowed with an evil fire. 'Then you will face the wrath of Omega,' the great voice roared. 'You and the miserable humans who accompany you here. Do you value their lives, Doctor? Do you value your own?' With a shock of surprise, the Doctor realised that Omega's surroundings were affected by his moods. Instinctively he knew this was a valuable clue to the workings of this strange world.

71

A panel in the wall near Omega suddenly lit up, and complex symbols streaked across it. Meaningless to the Doctor, it was obvious they conveyed some message to Omega. Abruptly he said, 'Investigate and follow. Bring them to me—but do not harm them.' Turning to the Doctor, Omega went on ironically, 'You are more fortunate than I, Doctor. You have just arrived on my world—yet already you have human company to share your exile.'

The Brigadier spent a moment taking in the incredibly strange panorama that stretched before him. Then he straightened himself up, slammed the main door and marched back to the laboratory. Benton was standing by the TARDIS calling, 'Will you please *hurry*, Doctor?'

The Brigadier added his voice to the demand. 'Doctor, come out here at *once*!'

Doctor Two popped his head out of the TARDIS. 'I'm just trying to find my flute,' he said peevishly.

The Brigadier was in no mood to discuss flutes. 'Now see here, Doctor,' he spluttered, 'you have finally gone too far.'

The Doctor chuckled at some private joke. 'I think we all have. What's it like out there?'

'There's sand everywhere,' said the Brigadier indignantly. 'Nasty grey sand. We're in some kind of quarry. Do you realise what you've done, Doctor— you've stolen the whole of UNIT H.Q.'

'It's no use blaming me. I tried to warn you.'

'What am I going to tell Geneva?' demanded the Brigadier. 'We're probably *miles* from London.'

'We are indeed,' muttered Doctor Two. 'Light-years, more like it!'

The Brigadier wasn't listening. 'Tell you what, you two stay here and keep an eye on the place. I'll pop out and find out where we are. Back in a jiffy.'

Before they could stop him the Brigadier was off again.

'Oh dear,' said Doctor Two. 'Oh dear, oh dear, oh dear!'

Benton sighed. 'We'd better go after him you know, Doc.'

'I suppose you're right,' agreed Doctor Two. 'Hang on a moment, I'll just have another quick look for my flute.'

Before Benton could stop him, he popped back inside the TARDIS.

It was quite a time before he finally emerged, despite numerous appeals from Benton. When he did finally appear he was still sulking because he hadn't been able to find it.

'Never mind your flipping flute, Doctor,' said Benton forcefully. 'What about catching up with the poor old Brig?'

'All right, all right, I'm coming,' grumbled the Doctor. He and Benton walked along the silent corridors, opened the main doors, and stepped out. They saw the same panorama of grey sands that had greeted the Brigadier. But there was one difference. The building was surrounded by the blob-men. The faceless servants of Omega had come to fetch them.

7

Door to Freedom

The Brigadier strode briskly across the dunes, trying
to persuade himself that UNIT H.Q. had merely
transported to some lonely part of Norfolk on a very
nasty day. He wasn't having much success. They didn't
have dull grey sand in Norfolk, as far as he knew. Or
a permanently purple sky. Or a strange eerie quality
of light, and an uncanny silence. Slowly he was being
forced to accept that he'd travelled a very long way.

As he trudged along, looking in vain for any sign of
life, the Brigadier gradually became aware that he was
being followed. A shadowy figure was trailing him
through the dunes. The Brigadier drew his revolver.
Waiting until a particularly steep dune loomed ahead,
he sprinted round the base of it, and doubled back
in his tracks. Dropping to the ground, he wriggled up
to the top of the dune, and peered over the top. A
figure stood looking ahead, obviously puzzled by the
Brigadier's disappearance. Rising to his feet the Brigadier aimed his revolver and shouted, 'Raise your
hands!' The figure whirled round, and the Brigadier
found himself staring down the muzzle of a double-
barrelled shot-gun.

The gun was held by a wiry middle-aged man with
a wrinkled weather-beaten face. A country man's face.

The Brigadier stared at the man. There was something familiar about him. 'Hollis!' he said triumphantly. 'You're Arthur Hollis, the game warden chap. The first one who disappeared.' He holstered his revolver. 'I'm very glad to see you, Mr. Hollis. Perhaps you can tell me what's going on here?'

Hollis gave him a suspicious stare. 'Your manoeuvres, innit? Thought you'd be telling *me*!'

'Manoeuvres?'

Hollis waved an arm. 'All this. Box came down, see? I touched it and—here I am. All different. Only the Government mucks things about like that.'

The Brigadier rubbed his forehead, realising that Hollis thought he was caught up in some kind of military experiment. 'No, Mr Hollis, you've got it all wrong. The fact of the matter is . . .' The Brigadier realised that he didn't actually *know* what the fact of the matter was himself, and changed his tack. 'I'm just as much in the dark as you are. All that has happened is the result of some kind of hostile force.'

'Oh ah? What force?'

'We won't go into that now,' said the Brigadier hurriedly. 'Just take my word for it. Tell me everything you've seen since you've been here.'

Hollis scratched his head. Self-expression wasn't his strong point.

'Well,' he said, with a mightly effort, 'there was two others turned up in a dafty motor, like. Tall white-haired feller in a fancy get-up, and a tidgy little gel.'

'The Doctor!' said the Brigadier excitedly. Then he

paused. He'd just left the Doctor, back at the strangely transplanted UNIT H.Q.

Could Benton's story be true after all? *Were* there two Doctors? Dismissing this problem for the moment he said, 'Go on. What happened to them?'

'Them blobby things got 'em. Them and another feller. Didn't get me though. I'm used to moving quiet. I followed 'em see . . .' Suddenly Hollis broke off, and flung himself down, motioning to the Brigadier to do the same. They wriggled round the side of the dune, and Hollis pointed. 'That's them. That's what I meant.'

The Brigadier saw the Doctor—the one he'd left at UNIT H.Q.—and Sergeant Benton. They were being herded along like sheep, surrounded by a circle of the blobby creatures. The Brigadier realised that if he hadn't gone off and got involved with stalking Hollis, he would probably have been captured himself. Instinctively he moved to go to the rescue, but Hollis's hand on his shoulder pressed him down.

'Hold on now. No use rushing 'em. I know where they're bound. We'll follow 'em.'

Keeping their distance, the Brigadier and Hollis trailed after the little group. They followed them on the long journey through the dunes, up to the point where the grey sand levelled out into a plain. Not daring to leave the shelter of the dunes, they watched helplessly as the little party went through the great brass gates which opened at their approach and clanged shut behind them.

'Well,' said Hollis. 'Now what?'

For the first time in his life, the Brigadier had a

moment of utter panic. By now he was so disorientated by the rush of sudden happenings that he simply had no idea *what* to do next. Then his instincts and training reasserted themselves. Whatever mad world he had tumbled into, he was a military man, and he would react in the correct military manner. 'First we'll do a recce,' he said crisply. 'Then we'll mount a surprise attack. Mr. Hollis, you will consider yourself under my orders.'

For a moment Hollis stared at him mutinously. But back in World War Two, he had been a soldier himself, and the Brigadier's level stare and clipped voice brought back long-buried memories. Clumsily he shouldered arms with his shot-gun and said, 'Righto, General!' The Brigadier nodded and, followed by his one-man army, began moving cautiously around the castle.

Inside, the Doctor was doing his best to reason with Omega. He was treading very carefully, more than a little hindered by his own awe of that legendary figure, very conscious of the way that Omega's powerful yet unstable mind could fluctuate between a rather ironic amiability one minute, and sudden terrifying rage the next.

'You yourself admit,' the Doctor was saying in his most persuasive voice, 'you cannot always be sure of controlling the matter-anti-matter reactions. If you find you cannot reverse the energy drain you have created through the black hole, the very fabric of the Universe could be torn apart!'

Omega's terrifying laugh boomed through the

brazen hall. 'What if it does? It will make an interesting spectacle.'

The Doctor was appalled by the callous egoism of Omega's response. Desperately he sought for some lever to move him. 'If that happens, then you will be alone forever.'

The great voice took on a note of sonorous gloom. 'I am used to solitude. If I cannot have my freedom, I shall have my revenge. I shall be satisfied.'

The Doctor made a final attempt. 'You have been unjustly treated, greatly provoked. No-one denies that. Undo the harm you have done and you can resume your place on the High Council. I will plead for you . . .'

The Doctor knew at once that he had made a serious mistake. The room darkened, thunder rumbled threateningly round the great hall, as Omega boomed, 'You will plead for me? You would do better to plead *with* me—for *them*.'

'You could have your freedom again . . .'

'Power is the only freedom. There will be no bargains with those who betrayed and deserted me. You are here for a reason, Doctor . . . I shall take you to the Flame of Singularity!'

The Doctor frowned. Once again this hint that he featured in Omega's plans. Before he could enquire further, they were interrupted. The doors clanged open and two figures entered, one large, one small, herded by a menacing circle of blob-men. Sergeant Benton, and the Doctor's other self. With a flash of irritation, the Doctor saw that the little man was looking round him with cheerful interest, like a tourist on a sight-seeing trip. Didn't the fellow take anything seriously? The Doctor found it difficult to realise that this scruffy, rather comical figure was an earlier version of himself. He felt this second Doctor was like a sort of younger brother, with a number of rather irritating mannerisms that he himself had outgrown.

The Doctor and Benton were both tall men, and Omega topped them by several feet. The unassuming figure of Doctor Two seemed positively dwarfed by the tall figures around him. Yet he was studying the huge robed figure of Omega with interest, peering up into the savage metal mask with an expression of polite anticipation, like someone meeting his host at a party.

There was a note of scorn in Omega's voice. 'Who are you? Why are you here?'

The Doctor saw Doctor Two about to open his mouth, and hurriedly answered, 'Oh, they're nobody. Probably just a couple of innocent bystanders, scooped up by that blundering jelly-organism of yours . . .'

'The organism was programmed to seek out a Time Lord,' said Omega slowly.

'Well it didn't do very well, did it? Two perfectly innocent people were transported,' said Doctor Two cheekily.

Omega obviously didn't care for any criticism of his works. 'Those were early errors, when the organism was newly arrived. Later they were corrected.' Omega stared down at the two new arrivals, and they stared back up at him. He looked from Benton to the second Doctor. 'Can this be a Time Lord—or *this*?'

Doctor Two seemed rather stung by the scorn in Omega's voice. 'Appearances aren't everything, you know,' he said indignantly.

'Strange—you do not fear me. Approach!'

Obediently, Doctor Two walked up to stand beside his other self. Omega considered them thoughtfully. Both Doctors could feel the pressure of that enormous intelligence bearing upon their minds. 'Can it be,' the deep voice rumbled, '*two* Time Lords? The *same* Time Lord? The High Council must be desperate indeed to transgress their own Time Law.'

Doctor Two coughed discreetly. 'Are you sure you're not mixing me up with someone else? You see, I'd just dropped in on some old friends when a horrible great blob of jelly . . .'

Omega's voice broke like a peal of thunder. 'Silence, while I consider this attempt to trick me. I should have known the High Council would attempt some pathetic deception. Did they think your two minds would be a match for mine?' Angrily, Omega began to pace up and down. 'I must decide what shall be your fate!'

Doctor Two sidled up to his other self and nodded towards Omega. 'Touchy chap, isn't he? I'm afraid I seem to have upset him!'

The Doctor looked down at him in despair. 'Do you realise who that is?' Rapidly he explained all he had learned since his arrival.

Even Doctor Two seemed impressed. 'Omega? Is it really him? I say!'

Omega strode back towards them. As if on some unspoken command, a circle of blob-men stepped from around the walls and surrounded them. 'Take them! Imprison them with their friends.'

Doctor Two was again indignant. 'Imprison? I say, that's a bit much. We've only just arrived . . .'

'Oh do be quiet!' snapped the Doctor. The blob-men herded Benton and the two Doctors away. Omega stood brooding, alone in his great hall.

The Brigadier and Hollis had completed their reconnaissance, but it had done them little good. A complete circuit of the castle, most of it wriggling on their stomachs, had revealed that there was only one way in. Now they were back at their original vantage point, just in front of the great brass doors. The Brigadier nodded towards them. 'There's only one thing for it.'

Hollis looked at him sceptically. 'Oh ah?'

'Take 'em by storm,' said the Brigadier briskly. 'Full-scale frontal attack using all the military resources available.'

'And what does that mean?' asked Hollis in his slow countryman's drawl.

The Brigadier gave him a rueful grin. As a young subaltern he had often dreamed of ending gloriously in some forlorn hope. Now it seemed he was to have his chance. 'That, Mr. Hollis,' he said gently, 'means you and me!'

The bare cell was uncomfortably crowded now. Jo, Tyler, Sergeant Benton and both Doctors. The atmosphere wasn't helped by the furious arguments raging between the last two.

'I tell you,' the Doctor was saying exasperatedly, 'I had a good chance of winning him over. Then you turned up, and he started treating me like an impostor.'

'Well so you are, in a way,' said Doctor Two annoyingly. He was thoroughly tired of being harangued by this tall, elegant version of himself. If that's what he was to become, he thought illogically, he'd sooner stay as he was. 'Although, in another way,' he went on, 'we're both impostors? Or is it neither of us?'

'Oh do stop wittering on while I'm trying to think,' said the Doctor.

Doctor Two glared at him. 'There's no need to be so unpleasant, you know!'

Jo looked at Benton. 'They're getting worse,' she announced loudly. 'They were *supposed* to help one another.'

Benton nodded severely. 'That was the idea.'

A sudden silence fell. The two Doctors looked at one another rather sheepishly. The Doctor rubbed his chin. 'It's possible I may have spoken a little sharply,' he announced, looking at no-one in particular.

Doctor Two said placatingly, 'My dear fellow, not a bit of it.' In fact, as both Doctors were well aware, they were behaving badly because both were overwhelmed by the magnitude of the problem facing them, and neither had any idea what to do about it. In his various incarnations, the Doctor had found himself up against many terrifying enemies. With the exception of the Master, this was the first time he had found himself opposed by a fellow Time Lord. And in comparison to Omega, the Master shrank almost to a petty criminal.

'Er, tell me, old chap,' Doctor Two went on, 'what did you make of him—Omega?'

'Well, to begin with, I'd say he was confused.'

Tyler, who had been turning his head from one to the other of the two Doctors, like a spectator at a tennis match, said bluntly, 'Well, I know *I* am.' He pointed to Doctor Two. 'Who's he, for a start?'

'Me,' answered the Doctor simply.

'Come again?'

'Oh, ask Jo, there's a good chap.' Turning back to Doctor Two, he went on, 'One minute Omega talks about his freedom, the next he's threatening universal destruction. I don't think he knows what he wants.'

Tyler was not to be put off. 'Aye, but what about this place? I mean, a world of anti-matter, and us in it. How can it exist?'

Both Doctors started to speak.

'The singularity phenomenon, you see . . .'

'The phenomenon of singularity in fact . . .'

Both stopped at exactly the same time. They glared at each other. 'Do go on,' said the Doctor politely. 'I'm sure you understand it far better than I do.'

'Not at all, old chap. Older and wiser heads, you know . . .'

'Doctors!' said Jo severely. 'Simple answers please. And one at a time. Or you can take it in turns.'

Doctor Two said, 'I'm afraid it's not a simple matter, my dear. But roughly, very roughly, singularity is a—a point in space-time which can exist only inside a black hole. And we've come through a black hole into a universe of anti-matter, close to this state of singularity—where all the physical laws of the Universe break down completely. That's how Omega was able to create the world we're in now, by a fantastic effort of his will.'

'All that's a gross over-simplification,' said the Doctor rather unkindly. 'But it gives you the general idea.'

Doctor Two gave him a reproachful look. 'Omega has found a way of controlling singularity, using the vast forces which exist within this black hole.'

'Aye,' said Tyler impatiently, 'but who *is* this Omega? What's he up to?'

The two Doctors looked at each other. These were matters they would normally never discuss in the presence of outsiders. But here, inside the black hole, all normal laws seemed suspended.

'Long ago,' began the Doctor, 'my race, the Time-Lords, discovered the secret of Time travel. But to make it work, we needed a colossal source of energy. Omega provided that power for us, in an incredible feat of solar engineering. In the process he was, as we thought, destroyed. Instead he survived *here*, in a world he created for himself, in the universe of anti-matter.'

Doctor Two added, 'We owe him a great debt. His imprisonment was the price of our freedom to travel in Time.'

The Doctor took up the story. 'For untold years he was trapped here, brooding over his wrongs. Then his genius found a way to strike back at us. He created the light-beam, used it to send the jelly organism to reach into our world, started the energy drain from our universe into his.'

Jo's mind was reeling from the vastness of the concepts being discussed. It was Sergeant Benton who brought things back to scale. 'Listen,' he said firmly. 'I

84

don't follow a word of all this. But one thing I *do* understand. This bloke Omega is up to no good, and you've got to stop him.'

'The thing is,' interrupted the Doctor gently, 'we don't think we can.'

Jo was appalled. In all the time she had known the Doctor, she had never heard him admit defeat. Dimly she sensed there was something about Omega that seemed almost to paralyse the Doctor's will. She knew that somehow she had to give him back his will to fight. 'Nonsense,' she said briskly.

'But what can we *do*?' asked the Doctor.

Sadly, Doctor Two echoed him. 'Where can we start?'

'You can begin by getting us out of here,' said Benton.

The Doctors looked round the four walls of the cell. Once again there was no door. The entrance had appeared when they arrived, and as mysteriously disappeared once they were inside.

Jo wrinkled her forehead. 'Look if I understood what you were talking about, this whole world, everything in it, was sort of thought up, by Omega?'

Both Doctors nodded.

'Well, if he can think up a cell, why can't you think up a door? You're a Time Lord, aren't you? In fact you're *two* Time Lords. Surely your wills combined are a match for his? Why do you think the two of you were sent here?'

'It *might* work,' muttered the Doctor.

'If the combination of wills *multiplies*, rather than

just doubles,' said Doctor Two excitedly. 'Let's try. Contact?'

'Contact!'

The two Doctors stared hard at the cell wall. Each in his mind, which was of course the same mind, formed the picture of a door. The wall was *not* blank. There was a door . . . a door . . . a door . . .

Jo, Benton and Tyler looked on anxiously. Suddenly, faintly, there *was* a door. It grew more and more distinct. And then it was there—an open door in the hitherto blank cell wall. Their road to freedom was open.

8

Escape from Omega

Confronted with freedom, everyone realised they had no very clear idea what to do next. Benton moved towards the door. 'Come on, then, let's get out of here.'

The Doctors exchanged glances, then nodded; for once in accord. 'You take Jo and Dr. Tyler out of here,' Doctor Two told Benton. 'See if you can get back to the TARDIS inside UNIT H.Q. We'll meet you there.'

Jo looked up at them worriedly. 'What are you going to do?'

Doctor Two gave a determined scowl. 'We're going to do what you suggested, my dear. Look for a way to defeat Omega.'

'You see,' said the Doctor, *her* Doctor, 'if our theory's correct, somewhere in this castle is the actual Point of Singularity, the centre of all Omega's power. If we can find it, gain control over it in some way, we'll be able to defeat him.'

Jo saw that both Doctors were cheerful again. She had given them the confidence to escape from the cell. But she had also inspired them to run into even more danger. She looked from one to the other, and realised there was no chance of changing their minds.

The little party slipped out of the cell, Benton, Tyler

and Jo, turning towards the great hall and the main gates, while the two Doctors headed the other way, deeper into the secret recesses of Omega's palace.

While Benton and his party had simply to try and retrace their steps, the two Doctors were heading into completely unknown territory.

They moved along endless brazen corridors, sometimes passing through huge vaulted chambers. The whole palace was empty, echoing, unfinished, as though Omega had tired of his creation the moment he had thought it into existence. They had no way of knowing that they were going in the right direction, yet both felt they knew the route. Often the corridors divided, but they never had doubts as to which path to follow. It was as though the Flame of Singularity was drawing them on.

Eventually they began to feel a kind of burning glow. It was like approaching an enormous furnace. They heard a low, roaring, crackling sound. The heat grew more intense . . .

Then they came to the door. It was not a door in any ordinary sense. Rather it was a curtain of flame, stretched across a mighty parabolic arch. The roaring and crackling sound came from beyond it. They looked at it. They looked at each other. 'Well,' said the Doctor, 'I think we've found it.'

Doctor Two gave a rueful grin. 'I almost wish we hadn't.'

'No use just standing here. Someone ought to go in.'

'Yes, they did, didn't they,' agreed Doctor Two unenthusiastically. He brightened. 'Tell you what, we'll toss for it.'

He produced his silver coin, but the Doctor put out a restraining hand. 'Don't bother,' he said wryly. 'I remember we tried that before. Wish me luck!' And with that the Doctor ducked through the curtain of fire.

Doctor Two waited, feeling slightly conscience-stricken. His double-headed Martian Crown had got him out of many tight spots, but perhaps it *was* a bit much to play tricks on himself.

Suddenly he heard the Doctor's voice. 'It's all right. Come through!'

Screwing up all his nerve, Doctor Two took a running jump through the fiery curtain. He was vaguely conscious that there was almost no sensation of heat. His feet skidded on the polished brass floor, and the Doctor caught an arm to steady him. 'Just take a look at that, old chap.'

Doctor Two looked. They were in another of the great chambers, smaller in diameter than the entrance hall, but far, far higher. In the centre, an enormous pillar of fire rose like a colossal fountain, disappearing into the recesses of the roof. Its ever-changing lights made flickering patterns on the polished brazen walls. They were at the Flame of Singularity.

Both Doctors gazed in awe at the spectacle. They knew of course that the Point of Singularity wasn't really an enormous flame. But that was how Omega thought of it, and in this world of Omega's creation, his thoughts were real.

They stood for a long time, hypnotised by the flame. It seemed almost impertinent to think of taming it, of bringing it under their control. Suddenly a figure walked through the curtain of flame behind them.

Omega stepped forward, towering over them both, and roared, 'I imprisoned you. How is it that you are free?'

Turning, the two Doctors locked their wills together, shielding each other from the terrible blast of Omega's wrath. 'We combined our minds against you,' said the Doctor calmly. 'Together we were able to overcome your barriers. You are not *all*-powerful, Omega—even in *this* world.'

Doctor Two spoke, and there was nothing comic about him now. His voice was stern, his manner imposing. 'Stop the energy drain, free us and our friends and we shall plead with the Time Lords to show you mercy. Otherwise, we shall combine our wills to destroy you.'

Omega's angry bellow threatened to shatter the brazen roof. The colossal flame flickered under his wrath. 'You threaten to destroy *me*?'

The Doctor was unimpressed. 'If we must, we shall fight you.'

Omega's laugh echoed around the room. 'You wish to fight the will of Omega? Then you shall!'

Suddenly they were—*elsewhere*. It was not so much that they moved, as that the room moved from around them. The Doctor blinked. He was standing alone, in the centre of an arena, rather like those used for games in the time of the Caesars. It was surrounded by high stone walls, unbroken except for a simple viewing stand, a kind of royal box. There, like some fantastic Roman emperor, stood Omega. Beside him, unable to move a muscle, was Doctor Two.

Overhead was the threatening purple sky of Omega's planet. Underfoot was the familiar grey sand. Into some corner of the Doctor's mind came the thought that, with the chance to invent a world, it was surely a waste of your opportunities to create such an unattractive one. From behind the Doctor came a grating sound. He whirled round. On the far side of the arena a door had opened. From it shambled— what? You could give it many names, thought the Doctor, as he backed away. Demon, Ghoul, Monster. Any of the horrors that rose from the black depths of the imagination. It was a good eight feet tall, humanoid in shape, apparently made of some substance like smooth black granite. The powerful limbs were knotted with muscle. Hands and feet ended in long evil talons. Small pointed ears clung to the ape-like head, and fangs gleamed inside the slavering mouth. The slanted eyes glowed a fiery red. As the thing came closer, the Doctor could smell the reek of sulphur on its breath. Suddenly something about that hideous face struck him as familiar. In a curious way, it looked like Omega. Naturally enough, thought the Doctor, since in a sense it *was* Omega. In this world Omega's thoughts and feelings were real, and this ghastly creature was an incarnation of all the rage and hatred that Omega felt towards the Doctor.

Gleaming claws hooked at the end of long arms, the monster shuffled towards the Doctor. He backed further away, and the creature moved after him with terrifying speed. The door through which it entered had disappeared, the walls of the arena were high and smooth. There was no escape. The monster sprang.

The Doctor was one of the few two-armed beings to have mastered the complex art of Venusian Aikido. He reached for the black shiny limbs, held, twisted, spun, and the monster flew howling across the arena and slammed into the steep stone sides. It twisted cat-like to its feet, and attacked again.

In the fierce struggle that followed, the Doctor was under one serious disadvantage. Nothing he did seemed to harm his opponent in the slightest, but there was no doubt as to its ability to harm him. Those claws and fangs were all too real, and if the thing once got a good grip of him, he would be torn to pieces. A slashing blow missed the Doctor's throat, but the creature's forearm slammed into his chest with enough force to send him crashing to the floor of the arena. The monster pounced, and landed on the spot where the Doctor had once been, as he rolled swiftly away.

From his place beside Omega, Doctor Two watched the struggle in powerless anguish. Locked in the grip of Omega's will he was unable to move or speak. He looked on helplessly as the Doctor ducked, weaved and dodged, throwing his monstrous opponent time and time again, only to have it bound back to the attack. Doctor Two could see that the end was inevitable. Time Lords had immense strength and endurance, but they are not superhuman or immortal. They can tire, they can be hurt, and they can die. Doctor Two wondered what would happen to him if his other self were to be killed. Presumably he too would wink out of existence, and cease to be.

It was obvious that the Doctor was beginning to tire. His holds and throws were fewer and less successful. Soon he abandoned retaliation altogether, and concentrated simply on evading the monster's claws. His foot skidded in the sand, and the monster was upon him, pinning him to the ground with its enormous bulk, the clawed hands digging cruelly into his throat. As the grip tightened, the Doctor could see only the metal mask of Omega gazing pitilessly down at him.

'Destroy him!' Omega roared.

With a tremendous effort, Doctor Two managed to speak. 'No, Omega, remember why you brought us here—you need us. If you kill him you destroy your only chance of freedom. Alone, I cannot help you.'

There was a long, terrible pause. Omega did not speak or move. From the arena came choking sounds, and the exultant howl of the monster.

Suddenly, monster and arena vanished. Doctor Two found himself standing at Omega's side by the Flame of Singularity. The Doctor was on his back, face contorted, hands still trying desperately to keep the claws of the now-vanished monster from his throat.

Realising that the struggle was over, the Doctor got slowly and painfully to his feet. He straightened his clothes as best he could, and dusted himself down. He nodded coolly to Omega. 'Thank you. A most interesting demonstration.' Then he collapsed into Doctor Two's arms.

Omega laughed. 'See what becomes of those who defy the will of Omega. Serve me faithfully, Time Lord, if you would escape the same fate.'

The unimposing figure of the second Doctor nodded humbly, as he carefully lowered the Doctor's tall figure to the floor. 'Yes, of course, Omega. Tell us what you want and we shall obey your commands. But I'm afraid my, er, friend will need to rest before he is fit to serve you.'

Omega nodded, then turned away, and disappeared through the curtain of flame. As he knelt over the slowly recovering body of his other self, the second Doctor's usually mild spirit was burning with a savage resolve. They would destroy Omega if it was the last thing they ever did. With a sudden rueful grin, he thought that it very probably would be.

Although they did not know it, the ordeal of the two Doctors was the salvation of Jo, Benton and Tyler. Almost the whole of Omega's mind was taken up with the punishment of those who had dared to defy him, and there was little of his attention left for the three figures creeping along the endless metal corridors.

It was for this reason, the simple absence of Omega's attention, that the palace seemed so empty and deserted as they made their way towards the entrance hall. Scarcely believing their luck, they reached it at last. They could see the main doors at the far end. Just as they were crossing the hall, Omega left the Singularity Chamber and returned his attention to the castle, sensing immediately that the fugitives were trying to escape. The matter did not concern him greatly. The humans were of little importance now the two Time Lords were thoroughly tamed. But it displeased Omega to be defied, and with an almost careless thought he despatched his servants to recapture the prisoners. Then he returned to endless brooding upon his coming revenge.

With freedom almost theirs, the escaping trio were horrified to see blob-men running towards them from every direction. By now they were at the massive doors, and they began struggling desperately to open them. The huge metal doors opened inward, and there was no handle to give them a grip. They scrabbled at the central crack where the double doors met, but couldn't open them more than a few inches. The blob-men came nearer and nearer, their jelly-like surface glistening horribly. Jo felt she would scream if one of them even touched her. All at once the doors started to move—not because of their pulling, but because someone was pushing from the outside. Soon the gap was big enough and one by one they squeezed through it, first Jo, then Tyler, then Benton. Outside, they were astonished and delighted to see the Brigadier, revolver in hand, backed up by another, smaller man clutching a huge shot-gun.

The double doors were closing again of their own weight as one of the blob-men tried to come through. Hollis's shot-gun blasted it into glistening fragments, and before it could reassemble the doors slammed to.

'Make for the dunes,' urged the Brigadier. 'They'll be after us any moment.' He led them at a brisk jog trot away from the castle.

'Excuse me, sir,' panted Benton as he ran up abreast of him. 'How did you know we were trying to get out?'

The Brigadier chuckled. 'We didn't. Saw the doors moving and decided it was our chance to get *in*. What about the Doctor?'

'Still inside, sir. Told us to make for UNIT H.Q. and wait there for them.'

'Them?'

'There really *are* two of them, sir. You ask the others.'

The Brigadier gave him a look, but didn't pursue the matter.

'Probably our best plan anyway,' he agreed. 'At least we can have a shot at defending the place.'

They were in the shelter of the dunes by now, and there was still no sign of pursuit from the castle. The Brigadier and Benton paused to allow the others to catch up.

'Listen,' gasped Jo indignantly, as she puffed up to them. 'We don't *have* to sprint everywhere like a team of Olympic athletes. Bessie's here!'

'The Doctor's car? Where?'

Jo's face fell. 'I'm not sure. Somewhere near the sea, where we first met Dr. Tyler.'

Hollis spoke suddenly. 'I know it. I was watchin' you. Just you follow me.'

He set off across the dunes, and they all followed. Hollis's countryman's instincts for a landscape seemed to be in full operation, even in this strange world. He led them unerringly across the dunes, and in a remarkably short time they were looking down at the Doctor's car.

Eagerly, they ran towards it. The Brigadier jumped behind the wheel, Jo sat beside him, while Benton, Hollis and Tyler piled in the back. Jo settled down in her seat, remembering how she and the Doctor had found the little car, so long ago. She turned to the

Brigadier. 'Where are we making for?'

'UNIT H.Q.,' the Brigadier said cheerfully, as he started the car. He noticed Jo's astonished reaction and grinned. 'Don't worry, Miss Grant, it's a good deal nearer than you think.'

From the back of the car, Benton gave him a respectful tap on the shoulder. 'It may not be too easy to reach though, all the same, sir.' He pointed. The dunes were lined with blob-men. One of them raised a shapeless paw, and the ground exploded in front of the car.

Once again, the fugitives benefited from the fact that Omega wasn't giving them his full attention. He had programmed his servants to recapture them, and left the matter at that, withdrawing his attention. The blob-men were programmed to use the simple herding method that had always before worked with humans. Now, however, they were after a very different quarry. Thanks to the Doctor's many improvements, which included a 'Superdrive', 'Bessie' was not only a very fast little car, but a supremely nippy one. She could spin round in her own length, and hills didn't bother her at all. The Doctor always said that he could 'drive her up the side of a house', and in the next few minutes the Brigadier came very close to proving just that.

Flicking the 'Superdrive' switch, stamping down hard on the accelerator, and spinning the wheel, the Brigadier whizzed the little car up the side of the dune, weaving to and fro to dodge the blob-men, and the explosions caused by their pointing fingers. He was quite accustomed to remaining cool under fire and the bangs and flashes didn't bother him at all, especially when he realised that they were aimed to deter rather than destroy. His passengers clung on frantically as he dodged their pursuers and whirled 'Bessie' round like a souped-up dodgem car, avoiding the gesticulating blob-men and the flurry of explosions. With a final triumphant roar 'Bessie' shot clean over the top of a sand dune and disappeared from sight, leaving her attackers milling about in hopeless confusion.

Before very long, the car was drawing up in front of the UNIT building, which still sat perched incongruously in the sand. They screeched to a halt, and the Brigadier jumped out cheerfully. 'Enjoyed that. Very pleasant little drive.'

For the first time, Jo realised that UNIT H.Q. really *was* in Omega's world. 'How did that get here,' she gasped.

'A very good question, Miss Grant,' said the Brigadier. 'We'll discuss it inside.'

They trooped through the front door, and into the familiar building. The Brigadier locked and barred the door behind them and led the way to the Doctor's laboratory. It still looked bare, since the greater part of its furniture was distributed over the surrounding dunes, but the solid blue shape of the TARDIS sat reassuringly in its usual corner. Jo had assumed they would shelter inside, but when she tried the door it was locked. The Brigadier shook his head. 'Typical,' he said. 'Never mind, we'll do the best we can with this building.' He produced a set of keys. 'Sergeant Benton—check the armoury. All the heavy stuff you can find . . . grenades, bazookas—I think there's an old Bren-gun in there somewhere.'

Benton said 'Yessir' and rushed out. The Brigadier surveyed the others.

'I think a few explanations are in order,' he said.

Everyone started to talk at once. The Brigadier held up his hand for silence. 'We may be in a rather unusual situation, but we shall conduct this de-briefing in a proper military manner. We'll start with you, Miss Grant. What happened to you and the Doctor after you, er, disappeared?'

Jo frowned. It all seemed such a long time ago.

'Well,' she began, 'we woke up on one of those nasty grey sand dunes . . .'

*   *   *   *   *

The Temporal Control Room of the Time Lords was almost completely dark. The President of the Council sat before the one monitor screen that still showed a faint glow of life. He operated the controls with clumsy fingers—it was many hundreds of years since he had performed such a menial task. But now there was no-one else. The Junior Time Lord lay sprawled across the floor at his feet, and in the nearby council chamber the members of the High Council lay slumped across the table, drained of all energy, drained almost of life itself.

Hoping desperately that the tiny trickle of power remaining in the storage banks would serve his purpose, the President touched a final control.

A faint, fluctuating picture emerged on the screen, the proud, fierce face of a formidable old man. 'Well,' it said grumpily, 'now what d'you want?'

The President gave a gasp of relief. 'Our energy situation is critical, Doctor. The drainage through the black hole is affecting our life-force. You are our last chance. You *must* go through.'

'Me? Through the black hole? Certainly not!'

The President spaced out his words carefully, guarding his remaining strength. 'All three are needed to defeat Omega—two not enough . . . must be totality. I'll use our last vestige of energy to send you through. You must consent.'

'Oh very well. You'd better get on with it.'

A final movement of the failing fingers over the control console and the picture faded away. The President slumped face downwards across the console. Like his fellow Time Lords he was in a protective coma, only the tiniest glimmer of life-force remained. Unless the energy drain was halted soon, even that would be gone. So too would that of the other Time Lords. As the energy blight spread, it would destroy every living creature in the Universe, and then the Universe itself.

9

'All things shall be destroyed'

Beside a towering cascade of flame, the being who had planned the end of the Universe looked at the two Time Lords standing meekly before him.

'No doubt you have guessed why you have been brought here. What it is that I need from you?'

The Doctor, now recovered from his ordeal in the arena, said nothing. Doctor Two, apparently more anxious to please, nodded eagerly. 'Well, yes, er, of course. Well, that is ...'

His voice tailed away feebly. The Doctor looked down at him disparagingly and said, 'What he means is—no. We haven't the faintest idea.'

Omega sighed, resigned to the stupidity of all other beings in the Universe. 'You know, at least, that this world exists by the effort of my will—because of my control over singularity.'

'Very impressive,' said Doctor Two, rather like someone being shown a really good card trick.

Omega ignored him. 'In singularity, *everything* is possible. I can create whatever I wish by the exercise of my will.' He nodded towards the taller Time Lord. 'You have experienced the way I can exteriorise my thoughts, even my feelings!'

The Doctor rubbed his throat. 'I have indeed,' he agreed.

Doctor Two piped up again, 'I say,' he said foolishly, 'you mean you just have to think of something, rub your magic wand over there . . .' he nodded disrespectfully at the pillar of fire, 'and shalamy-galamy-zoop, there it is? I call that jolly clever.' A sudden thought seemed to strike him. 'You couldn't run me up a quick flute, could you?'

Omega glared down at him. The room darkened, the flame flickered, and a distant threatening rumble of thunder gave proof of Omega's mounting anger. The Doctor poked his other self sharply in the ribs, but the clownish little man seemed lost to all reason. He held up his hands, a little apart. 'Wooden thing, about this long, with holes in it.' He looked hopefully at Omega.

Omega's voice boomed out angrily. 'I shall tell you now of the task before you . . .'

'Well it's not much to ask, is it?' muttered Doctor Two. 'I mean, one little flute . . .'

This time the thunder filled the room, and the fountain of flame seemed to roar in sympathy. Hurriedly the Doctor said, 'Just ignore him, please. I'm afraid he's incorrigibly frivolous.'

Once more there came that sulky but quite audible mutter from the level of his shoulder. 'Just because *you're* not musical. Wasn't your flute, was it?'

The Doctor hissed, 'Oh do stop interrupting us.' Turning to Omega he said politely, 'I'm so sorry. Please continue.'

Omega's angry bellow seemed to shake the entire

castle. 'Continue? You face annihilation, do you know that? You, your entire Time Lord race, the Universe itself, and what do you do? You babble of flutes!'

The Doctor took his companion firmly by the elbow, and led him a little to one side. 'Give me a moment to talk to him, Omega. I will make him realise his folly.'

Omega roared, 'You would be wise to do so, for both your sakes.' He stalked closer to his pillar of flame, as if to commune with it.

The Doctor leaned over his other self and whispered urgently, 'Just what do you think you're doing?'

There was no hint of foolishness in the serious face that looked up at him. 'Testing his powers of self-control. Can't say I think very much of them.'

'I think I see what you're up to. Dangerous though. If you provoke him too far, he'll kill you. Kill us both!'

'Have to risk that,' whispered Doctor Two. 'That temper of his is his only weakness . . .'

Omega rounded upon them, suspicious of their lowered voices. 'Do you plot against me?'

The Doctor hurried back towards him. 'No, no, I assure you. I was simply telling my—associate to show more respect, to listen carefully to what you have to say.'

The second Doctor came and stood meekly beside him. 'Please go on, Omega. You were mentioning some task . . .'

Omega gestured towards the pillar of flame. 'Here is the source of the light stream along which you travelled.'

The Doctor nodded, remembering the streak of 'space-lightning' which had first shown up on Tyler's cosmic-ray device.

'I created it, I alone, Omega. Yet it is not enough. None of it is enough. I am trapped, as surely as I was when I first arrived in this desolation.'

Puzzled, the Doctor said, 'I take it you want to leave here? But surely, if you can transmit matter to and from Earth along this light-beam, you could transport yourself, well, anywhere?'

'So I imagined. No, Doctor, there was no escape! As long as I control singularity, I can make it do my will. Without my will's unceasing pressure, everything here would revert to chaos.'

At last the Doctor saw the full irony of Omega's predicament. 'So, the moment you abandon control, you cannot escape. And you cannot escape without abandoning control?'

The great masked figure bowed its head. 'That is your task, Doctor, both of you. To take over my burden so that I can escape. Only when the Time Lords accept me as their supreme ruler, will I consent to save their Universe.'

The two Doctors looked at each other, as the full horror of the situation dawned upon them. They were to remain, trapped forever in this appalling place, while Omega became the ruler of the Time Lords, using their power for his own lunatic ends.

A note of irony came into Omega's voice. 'My world does not please you? Then you may transform it, once I have taught you the trick—see!'

One wall of the Singularity Chamber faded away

to reveal a beautiful green landscape, rolling fields, orchards in blossom, great stretches made colourful with trees, grass and flowers. 'Just such a world did I create when I first came here. But the beauty and the colour demand much effort from the will. As thousands upon thousands of years roll by, the strain becomes too great.' As Omega spoke, the colour drained from the landscape, the vegetation faded away, until only rolling grey dunes were left. 'You will end, as I did, with the simplest elements—sand, sea and sky.'

After a moment the Doctor said, 'And what if we refuse your generous offer?'

'Then the light-beam will go on absorbing energy from the world of matter. You, not I, will be responsible for the destruction of the Universe. What is your answer?'

The Doctor opened his mouth to reply, but Doctor Two forestalled him. 'We will obey you, Omega. We have no choice.'

A golden throne appeared behind Omega and he lowered himself upon it. 'Come—remove this mask.'

The two Doctors approached. Now that Omega was sitting, the great metal mask was within their reach. 'You too will need such masks,' said Omega. 'Working with the light-beam has a slow corrosive effect, due to the acceleration of the particles.'

Omega's 'mask' was in fact a kind of metal helmet, similar in construction to that on a suit of armour. It covered both head and shoulders although the 'head' was made to be separately detached. The fact that the light-beam was so dangerous, thought the Doctor, explained the metal mask, metallic robes, the metal boots and gauntlets, with which Omega always protected himself.

As their fingers worked on the fastenings, the Doctors could not help wondering what sort of face they would find beneath it. If the corrosion of the light-beam had already started its work . . . As the last fastenings came free, they braced themselves and lifted up the head-piece of the helmet.

What they saw beneath it froze them both with pity and horror. With one accord they lowered the mask back into place. But before they could close the fastenings, Omega swung his head round angrily. 'Why do you not obey me?' he roared.

The two Doctors looked at each other in helpless silence. There was genuine sympathy in the Doctor's voice as he replied, 'We cannot, Omega.'

'There would be no point,' confirmed Doctor Two. 'Destroy us if you wish—but what you want can never be.'

Slowly Omega rose to his feet. He strode across to one wall, and waved his hand. Immediately the surface became smooth and polished, a mirror of bronze. Gauntleted hands fumbling a little, Omega lifted the mask from his own shoulders. He raised it high above his head. Beneath it he saw—nothing. Just empty space. With a great howl of anguish Omega replaced the mask.

Sadly the Doctor said, 'The corrosion has already done its work. Your physical being has been eaten away. There is nothing left of you—except your will.'

'It is not true,' bellowed Omega. 'I am! I exist! I am Omega, creator of this world.'

'Don't you see,' said the Doctor sadly, 'you can exist *only* in this world.'

Doctor Two nodded. 'You have built your own prison. You can never leave it.' In the little Doctor's compassionate voice the words had the sonorous ring of a judge passing sentence.

They watched as Omega swayed to and fro, grappling with the horror of his fate. Hands flung out in anguish, Omega became still. With a terrible deliberation the great voice rang out. 'If I exist only by my will, my will is to destroy. All things shall be destroyed. All things! All things!'

A great crack of thunder split open the roof, letting in a howling wind, which made the fountain of flame flare up wildly. Jagged cracks appeared in the metal walls. The floor beneath their feet seemed to flow like a metal ocean.

Omega reeled to and fro in the flame, filling the place with howls of maniacal laughter.

The Doctor was watching the spectacle appalled, when he felt a tug at his sleeve. 'Told you he'd got no self-control,' whispered Doctor Two. 'I think this is our chance, don't you?'

As the two Doctors ran along the metal corridors, the whole building seemed to heave and quake around them. No-one attempted to stop them as they made for the great main doors at a staggering run.

It was like being caught in a combined earthquake and thunderstorm. As they reached the entrance hall, they saw the doors buckled open, one of them hanging from its hinges. Outside was a night of howling storm, lightning streaked across the purple sky, and winds whipped the grey sands into swirling clouds. Gripping each other's hands they plunged into the darkness.

Only one thing saved them from being hopelessly lost as they ran through the ever-changing shifting landscape, eyes and mouths choked by the swirling sand, blinded by lightning, deafened by thunder. They were making for the transported UNIT H.Q., and that meant for the TARDIS. As Time Lords, they had a homing instinct for the TARDIS stronger than that of any homing pigeon. Lurching and staggering they stumbled on through the howling chaos.

The Brigadier looked out of the laboratory window and wished he was back in England. In fact he wished the whole building was back in England. They were on the outer fringes of the storm which centred on Omega's castle, but they could see the howling gale outside, and hear the rumbling of thunder.

Tyler, Jo and Benton were finishing a kind of picnic meal, raked up from the UNIT canteen. It was cold, of course, and since the power sources were literally cut off, mostly out of tins, but it had made them all feel much better. The walls of the room were lined with an assortment of weapons, which Benton had brought up from the armoury. All in all, the Brigadier was pretty well satisfied with his situation. If only the Doctor would turn up, they could all get in the TARDIS and go home.

Jo joined him at the window, carrying a pinkish piece of meat on the end of a fork. 'Where do you get your supplies from, Brigadier? I'll swear this bully beef was canned for the Boer War.'

The Brigadier inspected it solemnly. 'Nonsense. Best 1940 vintage! They don't make it like that any more.'

Jo gave him a look, and popped the lump of meat into her mouth, chewing vigorously. 'Storm seems to be easing a bit,' she said a little indistinctly.

The Brigadier nodded. 'Funny thing though— wind's dying down but the thunder's getting worse. Listen.'

Above the wind, both heard a series of crashes. They seemed to be moving closer. 'Thunder be blowed,' said the Brigadier suddenly. 'Those are explosions. Stand by, everybody.'

They all seized weapons from the selection around the walls. 'Seems to be coming from the front,' said the Brigadier. They moved along the corridors towards the main door.

Nearby, on the dunes, the two Doctors were thankful that the storm was easing. 'Not much further, I think,' said the Doctor, as they staggered to the top of yet another dune. As they came over the rise, he shouted, 'Look!' Lashed by the dying storm, the UNIT building lay before them.

Doctor Two tapped him on the shoulder. 'You look, old chap.' The Doctor turned. A line of blob-men was lumbering purposefully towards them.

'We're just in time,' said the Doctor. 'Come on, we'd better get inside.' They started to run down the slope. A line of explosions followed them. From the dunes ahead more blob-men appeared on every side.

The menacing circle of Omega's servants lumbered ever nearer. Explosions began to tear up the ground all around them. They were surrounded—and cut off from UNIT H.Q.

10

Return through the Flame

Just inside the main door, the Brigadier and his small army listened to the explosions.

'Sounds like a full-scale attack,' muttered the Brigadier.

Jo Grant, staggering under the weight of an anti-tank rifle, panted, 'Brigadier, maybe they're not firing at us at all. Maybe it's the Doctor . . .'

The Brigadier said, 'I'm going to check.' He unlocked and unbarred the door and opened it a crack. Peering out he saw two figures, one tall and one short, racing across the sand towards them, twisting and turning to dodge the explosions that erupted at their feet.

'It's the Doctor,' yelled the Brigadier. 'Covering fire, everybody.'

Just as the Doctors realised that their enemies had cut off their approach to UNIT H.Q., they saw the doors flung open, and a strange looking force emerge. It was led by the Brigadier, with a Sterling sub-machine gun. Behind him came Benton, cradling a Bren-gun without its tripod. Tyler had an anti-tank rifle, Hollis his shot-gun, and Jo Grant brought up the rear with a rifle that seemed almost as tall as she was.

Cupping his hands to his mouth the Brigadier yelled, 'Get down, both of you.'

The two Doctors flung themselves to the ground as something that sounded very like a full-scale battle broke out above their heads.

As fast as the blob-men came up, the UNIT party blasted them to pieces. Benton literally sliced one in two with his Bren, and was horrified when the thick legs continued running towards him for a moment, before toppling into the sand. Direct hits from grenades disintegrated the creatures completely. The machine guns and Benton's Bren sliced them into separate fragments which wriggled horribly on the ground as they tried to reassemble themselves.

Jo Grant's contribution to the battle was limited. The recoil from her rifle knocked her flat on her back as soon as she fired it. Hugging her bruised shoulder, she decided to remain an observer. Although she realised that the blob-men couldn't be killed—as soon as they were blasted to bits, those bits started coming together again—there was something horrifying about seeing them mown down. She was very glad when she heard the Brigadier yell, 'Cease fire! Run for it, Doctor!'

The two Doctors picked themselves up and sprinted towards the doors. Even as they did so, more blob-men appeared in pursuit. The Brigadier bustled everyone through the doors. He and Benton, reloading frantically, hung back and fought a rearguard action, blasting down the blob-men as they appeared and falling back along the corridor to the laboratory.

As they dashed inside they saw the Doctor waiting

by the open door of the TARDIS. He waved them in, and followed. Doctor Two was already at the control console. He closed the door, and set the force-field in operation.

For a moment the little party stood gasping for breath, waiting for the rattle of bullets and the roaring of explosions to die away from their ears. Tyler and Hollis were gaping around them in amazement, and the two Doctors were excitedly shaking hands and slapping backs with Jo and Benton. The Brigadier cleared his throat meaningfully, and everyone turned to look at him. 'Now, Doctor,' said the Brigadier sternly, 'I'd like some explanations from you.' He looked at the Doctor's tall figure, and at the smaller figure of the second Doctor standing at his side. 'In fact,' said the Brigadier, accepting the inevitable, 'I'd like some explanations from *both* of you.'

Omega stood brooding in his ruined hall. In his mind's eye he had watched the battle outside UNIT, and seen the Doctors escape into the TARDIS. In his present mood of bleak despair it mattered little to him.

'Fools,' he muttered. 'Soon you will leave your pitiful refuge and come crawling to me for mercy. And by that time, your Universe will no longer exist!'

'. . . So there you are,' said the Doctor. 'They can't get in—and we can't get out.'

'We're besieged,' concluded Doctor Two. 'If only I could find my flute, I could play you a little tune to pass the time.'

'We must be thankful for small mercies,' said the Brigadier.

'Doctor,' said Jo. 'Why can't we just clear off home in the TARDIS?'

The Doctor replied, 'Because for one thing, we've done nothing yet to deal with Omega's plan.'

Doctor Two went to the console and flicked controls. 'And for another, we're immobilised, locked here by the force of Omega's will.'

'So what will he do now?'

The Doctor shrugged. 'Nothing, I imagine. Just wait.'

Doctor Two nodded in agreement. 'He's already waited for thousands of years.'

The rest of the party looked at each other appalled. It was Tyler who expressed their thoughts. 'This TARDIS of yours is a real marvel, Doctor, but I don't fancy spending the rest of my life in it.'

A light began to flash over the TARDIS scanner.

The Doctor said incredulously, 'Someone's trying to get through.'

Doctor Two rushed to the scanner controls. 'You don't think it could be...'

'Who else?'

Sure enough, the blurred image of the third Doctor appeared faintly on the screen. The old man gave his two other selves the usual disapproving glare. 'Well, what's all this—a mass meeting?'

The Doctor glanced round the rather crowded TARDIS. 'We had to bring them all in here with us,' he said defensively. 'Nowhere else safe.'

The old man sniffed. 'In a pretty pickle, aren't you? Trapped in your own TARDIS indeed!'

'It's all very well for you to talk,' snapped the Doctor.

'Talk's all I can do,' interrupted the old man, 'and not too much of that. The transference isn't stable. So let's get on with it, shall we?'

'On with what?' asked Doctor Two.

'Putting our heads together and finding a solution —hey?'

Watched by all the others in the TARDIS, the two Doctors froze. Each had one hand touching the other's temples, one hand resting on the scanner screen. There was a moment's silence, while the air seemed to throb with mental energy. The two Doctors stepped back, looking at each other with sudden excitement.

'Then we're all agreed,' said the old man on the screen. 'Risky, but it *could* work. I wish you both the very best of . . .'

Abruptly he faded away.

The Brigadier looked at Jo. 'What was all that about, Miss Grant?'

'Another of their telepathic conferences, I think.'

'And the old chap on the screen—he wasn't . . . ?'

Jo nodded. 'I'm afraid so.'

'Three of 'em! I didn't know when I was well off!'

The two Doctors were laying plans.

'We'd have to switch off the force-field generator,' said the second Doctor thoughtfully.

The Doctor nodded. 'And that will leave us defenceless.'

Doctor Two nodded. 'We'll have to risk it, all the same.'

Working quickly, the Doctor began to disconnect a side-panel of the console, while Doctor Two switched off the force-field.

'What's going on?' demanded the Brigadier.

Without looking up from his work, the Doctor said, 'We think we've found a way to deal with Omega.'

Doctor Two, who was helping him to lift away the panel, gave a sudden yelp of excitement. 'Look—my flute. There it is, stuck inside the generator.' He was reaching to fish it out, when the Doctor stopped him. 'No, don't touch it. It's exactly what we need.'

'Oh no! Not my flute.'

'I'll get you another. I'll get you a million of 'em,' said the Doctor exultantly. 'Come on, let's get to work...'

From a storage locker, the Doctor produced a jumble of advanced electronic equipment. The rest of the party looked on baffled as the two Doctors worked furiously.

Jo sighed. 'Well, at least they're doing something.'

'Yes, but what?' demanded the Brigadier peevishly. 'And what's that wretched flute got to do with it?'

In an amazingly short time the task was complete. The end result was a sort of plastic casket, which seemed to glow slightly. Inside it rested Doctor Two's flute.

With painful politeness the Brigadier tried again, 'Do you think you might tell me, gentlemen, what all this nonsense means?'

The Doctor gave him a triumphant grin. 'It means,

Brigadier, that we can strike a bargain with Omega!'

'With a plastic box of tricks and a flute?'

Doctor Two chuckled. 'The box of tricks is a sort of portable force-field.'

'And the flute, in the circumstances,' said the Doctor solemnly, 'is very much more than just a flute.' He looked across at his other self. 'I say, how do we get in touch with him?'

Doctor Two went to the scanner. 'I'll send out a general call. He's bound to hear.' He twiddled the scanner controls, and said, 'Omega, we must speak with you. Can you hear us?'

After a moment, a blurred picture of Omega appeared on the screen. The cruel metal mask stared at them malevolently. 'Have the rats decided to leave their bolt-hole?'

The Doctor said, 'We have found a way to give you your freedom. Can you free the TARDIS so we can come to you?'

'You *wish* to come to me?' There was a note of surprise in the voice. 'Then you shall!' The picture faded. Doctor Two operated the controls, and the TARDIS dematerialisation noise began.

'It's working,' whispered Jo. 'Can't you take us home now?'

'I'm afraid not. We can go only where Omega wants us to go.'

The journey was a short one. When the TARDIS landed, they stepped out into Omega's Singularity Chamber, at the base of the great pillar of flame.

The castle was still in ruins, the metal walls cracked and buckled, the roof gaping open to the purple sky.

The Doctor knew that by simply willing it so, Omega could have brought it back to perfect repair. It was a measure of the depth of Omega's despair that he had not bothered to do even that.

The little party filed out of the TARDIS, the two Doctors in the lead, and stood waiting. Omega did not speak.

'We have come to help you,' said the Doctor boldly. 'We have devised a means to give you your freedom.'

Omega straightened up, and the great metal mask swung towards them. 'What is this? More trickery?'

'You must return our friends to safety. We shall stay to assume your burdens.'

Jo sobbed. 'No, Doctor.' But the Doctor continued as if she hadn't spoken.

'Do you accept our bargain, Omega?'

Omega gestured to the pillar of flame. 'They may leave. Let them give thanks that Omega is merciful.'

The Doctor turned to the little group. 'I want all of you to step into that flame. It won't hurt you. On the contrary, it will take you home.'

There was a murmur of protest. Doctor Two said gently, 'Please, do as we ask—or you'll spoil everything.'

The Brigadier took charge. 'Do as the Doctor says please. Mr. Hollis, Dr. Tyler.'

Scarcely realising what was happening, Hollis and Tyler stumbled into the pillar of flame and vanished. 'Benton, Miss Grant,' ordered the Brigadier. Jo struggled and protested, but at a nod from the Brigadier, Benton simply picked her up and stepped into the flame with her. The two of them vanished. The

Brigadier straightened his uniform cap, raised his hand to the brim in salute, stepped smartly into the flame and he too disappeared. The two Doctors were left alone with Omega.

Omega's voice boomed out. 'Well, brother Time Lords, I have played your game. I know there can be no escape for me—nor yet for you.'

The Doctor held out the casket. 'You can have your freedom, Omega. It is here.'

Omega took a step forward, as if he felt hope, in spite of himself. He looked down at the casket. 'What is this that you bring me?'

The Doctor said, 'The only freedom you can ever have.' A sudden ring of command in his voice, he ordered 'Take it, Omega!'

As if hypnotised, Omega reached out and took the casket. He stared at it in amazement, and started to open the lid.

The two Doctors began to edge towards the TARDIS...

Omega opened the lid, and looked inside. 'A flute?'

As his metal-gauntleted hand reached out for it, both Doctors started to run.

Omega's fingers touched the flute—and he and the world of his creation exploded into nothingness.

11

Three Doctors Minus Two

Perhaps because it was her second journey down the
light-beam, Jo Grant recovered more quickly this time.
She woke up, face down on a polished parquet floor,
her nose inches away from a government filing cabinet.
She looked round. She was back in the Doctor's
laboratory and the room was full of confused people
picking themselves up. The Brigadier, Tyler, Sergeant
Benton . . . The laboratory furniture was back too,
benches, stools, filing cabinets, all in their proper
places. She could see the familiar view through the
windows. The building was back where it should be.
Everything was back—except the TARDIS.

Panic-stricken, Jo demanded, 'The Doctors? Where
are they?'

Dr. Tyler answered her. 'They got us away first,
didn't they. They made sure of that. Before . . .'

His voice tailed off. Jo ran across to him. 'Please,
you've got to tell me.'

'Well, if my guess is right, that flute was uncon-
verted matter, *our* kind of matter. Omega and his
world—anti-matter. Put 'em together and—finish !'

Tears came into Jo's eyes. 'And finish for the Doctor,
too ?' She began to sob.

The Brigadier found he had a lump in his throat.

'Wonderful chap. Both of him,' he said, a little incoherently. 'Privilege to know him. Had his little ways of course—sometimes hasty words—faults on both sides . . .'

Before the Brigadier went on to say something he might later have regretted, the TARDIS materialised in its usual corner and both Doctors stepped out, beaming happily. 'Doctor,' roared the Brigadier, 'what the blazes do you mean by frightening us like that?'

* * * * *

The Temporal Control Room was ablaze with activity, every piece of equipment in full operation, Time Lords bustling about trying to catch up on their arrears of work. Before one of the screens stood the Chancellor and the President.

'A brilliant scheme,' the Chancellor was saying. 'Of course, you always had my full backing.'

'Of course,' said the President, with gentle irony.

The Junior Time Lord looked up. 'I think he's coming through now, sir . . .'

The old man on the screen peered at them. Despite his usual air of grumpiness, there was a twinkle in his eye.

'Our heartiest congratulations, Doctor,' said the President. 'Total success. Omega destroyed and the energy leak checked . . .'

'More than checked,' added the Chancellor. 'Converted into a new power source.' He indicated a nearby screen. Where there had once been the black hole was now an expanding blaze of light.

I'm glad you're satisfied,' said the old man acidly. 'Black hole into supernova—once again Omega has provided. You really ought to be grateful to him. Put me in touch with the rest of me, will you?'

At a nod from the President, the Junior Time Lord began manipulating the controls. The picture on the screen faded.

The President looked at the Chancellor. 'I think we should indeed be grateful, my lord. Not to poor Omega, whose end to some extent atoned for his crimes, but to the Doctor, who saved us all from extinction.'

'What reward would you suggest?'

The President was silent for a moment. He was remembering a trial at which he himself had presided, remembering the sentence passed on the Doctor. A change of appearance, and exile to Earth for an indefinite period...

'I think we both know, my lord,' he said. 'There is only one reward that would mean anything to the Doctor.'

*   *   *   *   *

The Doctor stretched an elastic band as far as he could then let it go. It sprang back against his hand and he sucked his stung fingers. 'And there you are, you see?'

His audience—the Brigadier, Jo, Sergeant Benton and Dr. Tyler—looked at him blankly. Jo said, 'Where?'

Doctor Two was perched cross-legged on the bench, looking at a mouth-organ, but without any real enthusiasm. He played a few bars of 'Oh Susannah', not very well.

A little crossly, the Doctor shushed him and explained, 'Omega's will was the tension in the elastic. When it let go, everything returned to its proper place. We got to the TARDIS just in time . . .'

The Brigadier winced as Doctor Two played another trill on his mouth-organ. 'And all that fuss about the flute?'

A little sadly, Doctor Two took up the tale. 'I lost it you see—and it dropped into the force-field core of the TARDIS. Then when we were all "converted"—so we could mix with anti-matter—it wasn't. It stayed in its original state.'

'We rigged up a portable force-field to keep it that way,' explained the Doctor, 'and once Omega touched it, that was it!'

'Big bang—and black hole into supernova,' concluded Doctor Two. 'Pity it had to be my flute. It had a lovely tone . . .'

Suddenly a plaintive bleeping came from the TARDIS. The Doctor said, 'Him again—it must be!' He rushed inside, followed by Doctor Two. A little hesitantly, the others followed them.

The face of the old man was already on the scanner screen, looking at the two Doctors. 'Only just made it, hey?' he was saying, not without a touch of gleeful malice. 'Well, the party's over now. Everyone back to their proper time zones. You young chaps didn't do too badly, I suppose. Though the first thing *I* would have done . . .' He faded abruptly away.

Everyone turned to look at Doctor Two. He stood

there for a moment, unimpressive as ever, smiling his
gentle smile. He held out his hands in a gesture of
farewell. 'Oh dear,' he said. 'So nice to have met you
all. Goodbye.' And he too vanished.

Jo gave a little cry of disappointment. 'Oh Doctor,
he's gone. And he was so sweet!'

The Doctor gave her a rather enigmatic smile. 'Yes,
he was, wasn't he.' He shooed them all out of the
TARDIS, and came out after them locking the
door.

The Brigadier looked round carefully, as if making
sure that the second Doctor was really gone. 'Nice
little chap, but as far as I'm concerned, Doctor, one of
you is quite enough. Come along, Benton, we've got to
get this place running again. We'll have to make a full
inventory. Everything's got to be accounted for.'

Benton rose to his feet obediently. 'Yessir,' he said.
Then he paused. 'Sir?—if anything *is* missing—where
do we say it's gone?'

'Come *along*, Benton,' said the Brigadier firmly, and
marched him away.

Tyler said, 'Well, I'd better be off too. Thanks for
the trip, Doctor. I don't think I'll write it up for the
University though!'

The Doctor sat perched on a stool, elbows on knees,
chin in hands, his face sombre.

Jo knew him well enough by now to realise that he
never found his victories a source of unalloyed pleasure.
Somehow there was always too much sympathy for
the defeated enemy. 'It's Omega, isn't it?' she asked.
'You're unhappy because you had to trick him?'

'I didn't *really* trick him. I promised him his

freedom, and I gave it to him. The only freedom he could ever have—utter annihilation.'

Jo respected the Doctor's scruples, but she didn't share them. As far as she was concerned the end of Omega was a thoroughly good thing. How could you feel sorry for someone who had planned to destroy the entire Universe?

A sound filled the room. It was like the TARDIS dematerialisation noise, only much quieter, and it came not from the TARDIS but from the laboratory bench in front of them. A complex piece of equipment was appearing, fading slowly up into view. To her surprise Jo seemed to recognise it—

The Doctor had been trying to repair something like it when she had first met him in this very laboratory. Ever since she had known him, he had been trying desperately to evade the sentence of exile passed by the Time Lords and get the TARDIS going again.

There was no doubt that the Doctor recognised the strange-looking object. He picked it up carefully, almost with reverence.

'It's the Time Lords! They've sent me a new dematerialisation circuit.' He clutched his head. 'And my Time Travel theory—it's all coming back to me. Don't you see what this means? They've revoked the sentence!' The Doctor rose to his feet and began striding excitedly about the laboratory. 'Think of it! All of Space and Time, to roam in as I please.'

'I *am* thinking of it,' said Jo. 'I suppose you'll be rushing off just as soon as you possibly can?'

The Doctor stopped his pacing. He'd been less than tactful, he realised, in showing his pleasure so openly.

As he looked at Jo's sad little figure, the Doctor realised something else. Now that the ability to take off in the TARDIS was once more within his power, he wasn't sure he *wanted* to go. He knew he'd miss his friends, Jo, the Brigadier, Sergeant Benton, and his life as UNIT's Scientific adviser. For the first time, in many years of wandering, he'd found something that could be called a home, and he didn't want to give it up. Not completely, that is. One or two little trips from time to time, of course . . .

He put his arm round Jo's shoulders and gave her a consoling hug. 'You surely didn't think I'd just go off and leave you?'

Jo looked at him suspiciously. 'Frankly, yes!'

'I couldn't do that even if I wanted to.' He held up the circuit. 'This has to be installed first—and that's a long and complicated job. The poor old TARDIS will need a thorough overhaul. It'll all take quite a while.'

'But you will go—eventually?'

'Tell you what, when the TARDIS is ready, I'll take you on a trip. Did I ever tell you about Metebelis, the famous blue planet of the Acteon galaxy? Lakes like great sapphires, mountains of blue crystal . . .'

Jo wasn't listening. A sudden worrying thought had struck her. 'Doctor, what about Mr. Hollis, the game warden? He didn't turn up here with the rest of us.'

The Doctor smiled reassuringly. 'Well, he didn't start from here, did he? Don't worry, Jo. I'm sure Mr. Hollis is back in his proper place—just like everyone else. Now, about our trip to Metebelis . . .'

It all ended very quietly, just as it had begun. Arthur Hollis picked himself up, looked around, and nodded in silent satisfaction. Grass, trees, flowers, and above all birds. The starlings were chattering indignantly, disturbed by his sudden arrival. A flapping sound made him look up. A silvery-grey balloon was tangled in one of the trees. No sign of an orange-coloured box, though, he noted thankfully.

Hollis picked up his shot-gun, checked it was empty, tucked it under his arm and set off for his cottage. As he drew near, he saw his wife standing at the garden gate waiting for him, and he quickened his step.

As soon as he was in earshot, Mrs. Hollis began scolding him affectionately. 'And where do you think you've been, Arthur Hollis? People here looking for you, scientists, soldiers and I don't know what. Told 'em you'd be back in your own good time. Where've you *been*?'

Arthur Hollis looked at his wife. She was one of the best, his Mary, but a terrible one to talk. Ran in the family; her mother and her sisters were just the same. Hollis himself had never been much of a talker. The thought of describing his adventures to his wife, and trying to answer her questions, filled him with horror.

He put his arm round her waist and gave her an affectionate hug. 'Wouldn't believe me if I told you, woman. Now then, supper ready?'

They went inside the cottage and the door closed behind them.

If you enjoyed this book and would like to have information sent you about other TARGET titles, write to the address below.

You will also receive:
A FREE TARGET BADGE!
Based on the TARGET BOOKS symbol—see front cover of this book—this attractive three-colour badge, pinned to your blazer-lapel or jumper, will excite the interest and comment of all your friends!

and you will be further entitled to:
FREE ENTRY INTO THE TARGET DRAW!
All you have to do is cut off the coupon beneath, write on it your name and address in *block capitals*, and pin it to your letter. Twice a year, in June and December, coupons will be drawn 'from the hat' and the winner will receive a complete year's set of TARGET books.

Write to:

TARGET BOOKS,
Universal-Tandem
Publishing Co.
14, Gloucester Road,
London SW7 4RD

If you live in New Zealand, write to:

TARGET BOOKS,
Whitcoulls Ltd.,
111, Cashel Street,
Christchurch

If you live in South Africa, write to:

TARGET BOOKS,
Purnell & Sons,
505, C.N.A. Building,
110, Commissioner Street,
Johannesburg

If you live in Australia, write to:

TARGET BOOKS,
Rical Enterprises Pty. Ltd.,
Daking House,
11, Rawson Place,
Sydney, N.S. Wales 2000

———————————— cut here ————————————

Full name...

Address...

....

....

Age.....\............................

PLEASE ENCLOSE A SELF-ADDRESSED ENVELOPE WITH YOUR COUPON.